THE INUGAMI MOCHI

Saddle Road Press
Ithaca, New York
saddleroadpress.com

Cover and book design: Don Mitchell

This is a work of fiction. Names, characters, places, and incidents either are the product of the author's imagination or are used fictitiously.

ISBN 978-0-9969074-0-8

Library of Congress Control Number: 2015953820

Books by Jessamyn Smyth

Koan Garden
Kitsune
Skaha
Gilgamesh Wilderness

v 2.0

THE INUGAMI MOCHI

JESSAMYN SMYTH

SADDLE ROAD PRESS

An Inugami (lit. "dog god") is a familiar spirit that looks like a dog and acts as a protective guardian. Inugami are extremely powerful and loyal, and they are known to carry out acts of revenge on behalf of their "owners." They can also exist independently...Inugami also have the ability to possess humans.

— *Edo Period Monster Paintings* by Sawaki Suushi

In the Oki Islands...It is believed that an *inugami-mochi* will be blessed with great fortune and success, and that favors granted by them will be returned with interest. However, in exchange the *inugami-mochi* are shunned by other people, and find it hard to get married; they must also be careful not to offend their *inugami* lest they receive its wrath, as unlike the *kitsune*, an *inugami* does not merely follow its master's wishes, but also acts on its own impulses.

— "Inugami" Wiki

Contents

A More Perfect Union

Dog catches Cecily standing unmoving in the middle of the living room, staring at the wall again.

It's fine as long as I keep moving, Cecily explains when she notices his observation. It's just that I finished everything too quickly today.

She sits down next to him, on the couch. Dog regards her kindly, as if to agree that it is a fine balance, this timing of tasks to run out only when it is late enough to sleep.

We had a nice walk, though, eh?

Dog agrees. A long one, in new directions; coyote marks, a swim, several pissed off chipmunks, one dead thing. He's happy.

Sorry, doggeleh. She pauses, appraising her hands. They are very clean. She appraises him: Oh, my god, look at your face!

Dog raises his ears, wondering if he has something stuck in his flews.

You're so beautiful you make a person's heart explode with joy just from looking at your face!

He lies back down, puts his paw on her arm. She says that a lot. He takes it in.

It's fine as long as she doesn't look in the mirror. That vaguely cat-like reflection, those eyes and everything in them; it hurts her, wasted as it is. She looks at the dog instead. He is very beautiful. He takes her in.

Some people just go out for dinner with friends, Cecily thinks. They laugh, drink too much, flush, tell stories, hug on the sidewalk, go home to whatever noises bounce best from their rafters, or pressed tin, drop-ceilings of that strange fiberboard stuff that inevitably falls out of its metal trim. In-laws. Lovers. House-mates. Children. Cecily wonders what sort of ceiling she would like best; decides, eventually, that she likes the one she has. Rough-cut lumber with sheetrock in between. She likes the word 'sheetrock.' It's so secure. She sleeps.

In the woods, Dog and Cecily find two dead things, partially digested. New trails opening up left and right. Bear scat. Horse prints. They step over frogs. She keeps moving, she grows thin, gains muscle, loses it, eats too much, doesn't eat at all. Spider webs cling to her face. She brushes them off. Pine needles smell like cedar at a certain time of year, she notices; in the early autumn, when the humidity hasn't quite gone but is going. She tries to remember what a cedar tree looks like, but all she can picture is a cypress bent in fierce wind; they are so elastic, cypress trees. They bend and bend, they rarely break.

She sees the biggest spider she's ever seen on the beaver dam they use to cross the brook. She wishes she didn't know spiders could get that big. It's better not to know. She throws a rock at it, misses. She doesn't like spiders.

When she puts on lipstick she looks at her lips; glances at mascara brush and lashes only. Parts. She dresses cautiously for work, stopping short of sexy; serious, slight funk visible around the edges. She teaches literature. Her students think she's cool. She directs the plays she writes. Dressing for rehearsals, she adds blue nail-polish, tighter pants, a lower neckline. Her actors think she's hot.

Once, she invited one of them to stay after a last rehearsal at her house. It had been awkward, loaded, which was not what she had expected: normally, they were easy together, but she found herself tangled by uncertainty every time she started to make an invitation. His cues were unfamiliar, she didn't know her lines. Finally, when discomfort reached comic proportions, she told him he was very difficult to read. He had laughed, relieved, and said she was, too.

"Am I?" She'd asked him, seriously wondering. It was not a way she had thought of herself: she feels transparent.

"Impossibly," he'd said, still laughing. "You're so damned beautiful and composed."

Composed, she had thought. What a strange word.

"Oh," she'd said. "Well. Would you like to come upstairs?"

She'd stepped into him easily enough, and his body welcomed her kindly. Their lovemaking left her more relaxed than she'd been, if still untouched; she'd thought of still lifes, marble, blocks of quartz at water's edge. In the morning, she'd sent him home with a companionable hug, vaguely regretting the fact that she knew she wouldn't want to do it again.

Dead thing on the floor when she goes to make coffee; a present from the cat. Dog points it out to Cecily, concerned she shouldn't step in it.

Thanks, poochelah, she says, and sweeps it into the dustpan, takes the pan outside, and like a Scottish stone-thrower, hurls the eviscerated mouse.

A sailing corpse cloud-busts: it breaks apart the sky, then hits a branch and spins, gravity takes over, it rustles the brush where it lands.

"I'm sorry, mouse," she says. She always says that to the bodies. Dog gazes out over the brush to where the dead thing fell.

Don't you go roll in that, Cecily says.

Dog looks at her, profoundly impugned. He's pissed because the actor, like everyone else, didn't stay. He loves Cecily, but he's a pack animal, and she is too few. She can't help it. He turns his back, walks ostentatiously away from the corpse, as if he would never roll in something dead.

Oh sure, mister, Cecily says to his departing tail. Remember the deer?

She has deer eyes, her lovers say. She supposes this is possible; her mother does, and her eyes are not unlike her mother's. She dreamt once that she was a deer, stripping the velvet from her antlers on the body of the giant maple in her woods, running with a herd of thousands; each body a ghost, each ghost a history.

When Dog found a deer dead only a few days, he came back to her streaked with yellow and green pus, freshly decomposed flesh clinging to his collar. The sharp reek made her eyes water. She lifted him up and climbed into the tub, his collar, her streaked clothes, still on, washing and washing, deer cycling down the drain, clockwise. They were both very clean when she finished, but she imagined the smell clung, for days.

Sitting in the grass, Dog returns to the subject of the actor.

He can sing Irish ballads from memory, Dog suggests.

He drinks too much, Cecily says.

He's a scientist-theatre-geek-person. We like those.

He's unemployed; he doesn't know what he wants. I've dragged that weight before, Cecily states. He's too young, anyway.

He chased me around the yard, and threw the ball, Cecily.

That's true, doggelah, Cecily says. He did.

He's nice.

You're right, he's great. Just not it.

How do you know? Dog wonders.

By the pitch. And how it resonates. Or doesn't.

They observe the clouds.

I'm sorry, ruggelah, Cecily says. Really.

Dog makes no comment.

At work, she asks her students to write her a paper about critical thought. She waxes rhapsodic about what that is, to do, how it is all that matters, in the end. She explains narrative voice, point of view. She asks her students what evidence is in the text; she says everything is intentional. She praises the life-sustaining qualities of words strung together, one after another, to break apart the sky.

She used to live in a democracy, but doesn't anymore; the fact that no one seems to mind terrifies her, but she keeps moving. The radio strings together words in ugly, binding ropes.

Her students give her papers that say they had never thought about thinking critically before, but now they feel so free. They can change their lives. Break patterns. Understand things, finally. Be informed citizens. She cries, unexpectedly, reading these papers.

The radio drones. A terrorism expert says Hussein when he means Bin Laden and the reporter corrects him, gently, politely; the expert, chortling, concedes his mistake.

Barely relevant, the names of our excuses. Cecily thinks. We are barely pretending, now. It is an inside joke.

Dog groans on the couch. Cecily turns the radio off, decides they should go for a walk instead of doing errands. The tank is on empty, but she doesn't feel like buying gas. She thinks about small rebellions, and picks up the pad of paper on the counter to make herself a note to assign George Orwell's essay "Why I Write" to her freshman sections. She tears off the grocery list on the top sheet, but an ink outline of a woman's body is revealed where the clean page she wants should be. A shadow-outline, impressed through paper now gone.

The missing page had hung on her last love's wall, until it didn't anymore. A nude portrait left in substitution for the morning note on the kitchen counter. Dark ink lines suggesting arm, hip, breast; the particular squareness of her jaw and shoulders, the firm, downward curve at the edge of her mouth, the joinings and edges that created such desperate tenderness in Cecily. Faded now, but impressed still, the image shocks her, and visceral reaction takes place. Her eyes close tightly. Her stomach hurts. Something essential plunges inside her. Her hand shakes, holding the shadow. Her chest shrinks from echoing vast hollow to a narrow, constricted place that cannot get enough air. Old wounds ache, bruises invisible, but impressed: the suggestion of a shove, the particular insults and rages, a tear in Cecily's flesh that would not stop bleeding in spite of its smallness, the sensation of being thrown, of cringing from hands pounding the air behind her head.

She decides to throw the paper away, and finds she cannot: this shocks her even more than the appearance of ghosts, dead inside her, decomposing, too slowly. She puts the remaining image in the sideboard, out of sight.

Cecily stands in the center of the room, staring at the wall. Dog hurries over and throws his stuffed orca at her feet. He stamps his foot on it, to make it squeal.

Soon, love, she says, meaning it, but she does not move.

Dog pitches the orca, hard, at her knees. She picks it up absently, sets it aside, does the dishes. Bleaches the stove for good measure, even though it's already clean. Finally, puts on her hiking boots; Dog dances when he sees them.

There is a porcupine trundling the path ahead of them. Heel to me, Cecily hisses. Dog quivers from nose-whiskers to ankle-feathers, but he heels, and the porcupine disappears noisily, without incident.

How good you are, Cecily says, when the danger has passed. Okay, run.

Dog stands still for a moment, listening for a squirrel upon whom he can vent the missed opportunity: he finds one, trees it in a blur of fur. It screeches and chitters. An acorn bounces off Dog's head, with a violent thunk.

What a scary boy, Cecily says. He has never been quilled. She hopes he never is. The barbs do more damage on their way out than on their way in: she doesn't want him to know this. It's better not to. She throws a stick. When Dog leaps a fallen tree to catch it, his beauty steals her breath. He can fly.

Once, while walking a friend's Rottweiler, the dog realized before Cecily did that an apparent pile of leaves under a tree wasn't one; she was unable to stop him before he got a face full of quills. With pliers, she'd managed to get all but one out. The last quill had gone so deeply into his lower gum, just under his canine, that it snapped off when she pulled it. She had poked gently at the broken shaft, to see if she could get a grip, holding the moaning dog's mouth open and crooning to him, but he'd pulled away and placed his jaws around her wrist, the points of his teeth just grazing her skin. Holding her hand still, he'd rolled his eyes and looked at her apologetically.

"Can't take any more, sweet boy?" She'd asked him, unmoving, and a single tear had rolled from his eye over his bleeding cheeks. "Okay, brave, good dog. No more." She put the pliers down.

He had let her wrist go, then, and put his head in her lap. She'd stroked his ears and given him ice cubes to suck.

The quill had come out on its own eventually. Sometimes, they do that. They bear watching, though, because sometimes, they don't.

"How do you know when it's time to leave?" Cecily's sister asks on the phone. They have both been listening to the news. "I mean, seriously, how do you know what time it is?"

"I don't know if you ever do," Cecily says. "Sometimes you leave and regret it; you didn't need to, it would have made a difference had you stayed and fought. So the next time, you stay and fight, because if there is even a remote possibility that it makes a difference, you have to, right? The Bill of Rights, you say. Love, you say. And then you discover the time came and you didn't recognize it, now you are fenced in, it has become fatal, you will be lucky to slip out through the tunnel you dug under the barrier with your fingers, with a broken spoon, with a quill pulled from your own flesh."

Cecily had lived in Greece for two years, to study the three hundred and fifty year history of a Sephardic community eradicated in a few weeks of 1944, after a somewhat slower ascent from Nationalism to Fascism made genocide possible.

She'd struggled, learning the language, but after many months she had a dream in Greek and knew it was coming together, finally:

She dreamt she was standing in a red, icon-painted chapel with all her notes—the Nazi deportation schedules, a stack of Sephardic recipes, charts of blood relationships proving guilt, hand-painted photographs of a Purim play— clutched in her arms; she could barely keep hold of them, she had no hand free to light a candle. She heard her own voice asking the bleeding icons, over and over:

Πού είμαι; Τι ώρα είναι;

Where am I? What time is it?

Sometimes she still has that dream, or ones like it, and always in Greek. After that last love, the one she really wanted, nearly killed her, and no one listened, or heard only the parts they wanted to, she dreamt repeatedly that she was struggling upward through water that had nearly drowned her, or earth that had nearly suffocated her, and after vomiting the fluid or soil clear, she would hear her own voice rising like prayer: where am I? What time is it?

"With hindsight," Cecily says into the phone, "you can see you were foolish—running toward your own death, really—from the beginning. But at the time, you think fighting, reasoning, inventing narratives to explain it into something other than horror, something you can overcome, will make a difference. You have the wrong time. And you end up full of quills. It's only when you're pulling them out that you understand how badly you've been hurt, and how you might have avoided it."

"Quills?" Her sister says. "What's all this about quills? I'm talking about moving to Canada."

"The point," Cecily says, "is even if you're paying attention, reading signs, you still don't know what time it is. Only history knows that."

"So how do you choose between fight and flight?" Cecily's sister asks.

"I don't know," Cecily says, after a while. "But don't flee before the election."

"Of course not," her sister says.

They hope it matters, this voting thing.

Sometimes it's better to hope.

What about the Scrabble champion? Dog asks Cecily. They are sitting in the grass, at dusk.

I will inevitably remind him of his mother. He has warned me of this, Cecily replies.

The actress?

Pothead.

The CEO?

Passive aggressive, manipulative, dishonest.

She loved me, Dog says.

Yeah, Cecily says.

She brought me pig-ears.

I know, poochy-love. I'm sorry.

She didn't make you happy, though, Dog concedes. You cried every time she touched you.

Yup, Cecily agrees. Because she wasn't you-know-who. Maybe it was just too soon. Or you know, maybe I was out of my mind.

Dog sighs, says: it's true that she was unpredictable in her loyalties.

Very, Cecily says. And I made her feel insecure, so she fought for control.

We've done that before, Dog says.

Yup, Cecily says.

We don't like that.

Nope, Cecily says. Sometimes it's better to be alone. To flee.

Dog, who loves uncritically, isn't sure about this last point, so he leans on Cecily's shoulder. She puts her arm around him. They watch the moon rise, fat and brilliant.

Cecily asks Dog if he remembers how to howl. He doesn't answer.

The coyotes do it for them: an aria first, harmonized, a chorus, finally. They are so many.

Satan's Kingdom

Old Vernon Road winds through elegant swamps of nesting eagles, herons, apparent miles of lily pads, the road itself a bridge between bodies, water on both sides.

Cecily stops her car for a painted turtle, brilliant bands of blue on its neck. Dog twitches in the seat next to her. Watching the turtle's ambling progression across potholed macadam from one amphibious world to another, she remembers a different bridge through water: suspended three feet below the water's surface, made of algae-coated iron, and in the middle of the ocean.

She'd had to cross this, for some reason, knowing the whole way that the moment a wave came she was lost. She'd slid her feet carefully on the slippery metal, trying to remain in constant contact, but the inevitable wave came and hit her chest-high: she'd been swept, instantly, sideways and down, down for apparent miles, to sand and hulking shapes of seals and whales, sunken ships.

She had returned to bone on the way down, Sedna again, a skeleton at the bottom of the ocean waiting for an endless procession of shamans to come comb her hair, then leave her to be chewed by sharks, worn down by shifting sand.

When she'd come out of that one, she'd been weeping and thin for a while, but knew it wouldn't last: the surface's call was too strong now.

The turtle achieves the side of the road and Cecily and Dog weave the car forward through fields of toads, leaning left and right to will the tires clear of their crowding bodies. Water hangs; the air is soft-focus with it, the ground a system of miniature lakes. Clumps of mist collect in neat bales everywhere there is a dip. Robins litter the road, spear toads with their beaks. She parks at the trailhead. Foolishly, they have come to Satan's Kingdom Wildlife Management Area at dusk after a vast storm: outside the car, a cloud of mosquitoes rushes them, darkening the air with their bodies.

Dog, whose anticipation of forest has quivered his flanks for miles now, is inundated. He shakes and shakes, they make for his eyes.

Move fast now, she says, and as they jog into the woods she buttons her sweater all the way up, takes down her hair to cover her neck, peels a maple switch from a tree and fans the bugs clear. She holds her belt-loop to keep her pants up and runs, Dog keeps a busy pace, but the bugs win. They will soon be a pint lighter.

The trail itself is sodden, pooled. She hops around the largest bodies while Dog plows through, puddle-stomping. The air is liquid New England: green and gold made scent, pine needles composting, maple overhead and underfoot, moss, swamp, loamy earth and metallic granite. She breathes it in through a net of her hair to keep bugs out of her lungs.

It's good to be on the surface, she wants to breathe again.

A bright flame slithers across the path. Then another, and another. Tens of them. Scores of them: the ground is afire.

She watches the flames, she watches her feet. Ember-bright efts carpet the ground. Dog steps on one by accident and jumps: the creature twitches, shakes it off, keeps going, brilliant and weirdly sturdy.

"Hello," she says, and bends to a small, orange body. Dog, peering over her knee, inspects the creature carefully. The eft inspects them back. "Medieval alchemists thought you were the elixir of life." It seems a polite thing to say. She extends her hand, and the juvenile spotted newt nudges her with its orange nose. "They said you lived in the flames and transmuted their metals for them. Sometimes they called you basilisk." It nudges her again. "Is it true that you breathe through your skin?" The eft puts one foot up into her palm for a moment, then heads off in a different direction. She watches it wriggle out of sight. Though they aren't, the flame-bodies at her feet seem absurdly soft, terrifyingly vulnerable.

Dog swipes his paw over his face, blanketed by mosquitoes. She lines his collar with ferns, a waving shield in front of his eyes. They have bitten her too, fiercely. She calls him onward, fans the maple switch around both of them. They run up a steep hill. She has learned it is easier that way; given less time to think about it, muscles obey without complaint, leave biting torment behind.

At the top of the slope, a clearing. Cecily remembers another glade in another wood, where two young griffins flailed about on the ground. Small for mythical creatures, about the size of large Rottweilers. They did not understand why they could not fly. They stared at her and scratched the ground with lion legs, eagle talons. They raised their beaks to the sky and pierced the air with screams.

She looked around for something useful, saw a sphere of red granite. She picked it up and rolled it gently toward the animals, suggesting play.

One of them lunged at the ball and attempted to rend it with raging talons. It did not even try to use its wings; they hung limp. She found a second sphere, this one black as obsidian, and rolled it. The other griffin screamed again, its beak wide and gasping to the sky.

They scratched and tore at the stones. Myths in an earthbound trap, their panic and rage would tear anything that came near. Her heart broke for them.

"You have to fly," Cecily says aloud. "I can't help you."

She closes her eyes, reopens them, walks away.

Dog follows. He looks back once at the clearing where two wild turkeys squawk about something that is distressing them, then looks to her.

She says: They'll figure it out, angel. Remember? They just have to remember.

The spheres Cecily dreamt have since sprouted green, wildflowers sprung up around them. They have become relics.

Here, she says to Dog, when they reach the stone overlook at the crest, the sudden drop. Here we are.

She remembers uncoiling and stretching, light pouring from her, soaring; cutaneous respiration sighed through the insides of her elbows, fingertips, throat, the backs of her knees. I'm a basilisk, she'd said, and laughed: the sound bounced from the ceiling and the walls like wind chimes. She could fly. She had frightened the man who had come to her bed, who had come for shamanic rites. When he combed her hair, it would not be still; oceans of hair spread across his knees, eddied at his ankles. She would not be serious. He drowned in her pleasure. She laughed and laughed.

And then all was still.

A sheer face falls to old quarry waters below, to green and black depths.

Myths accrue in this under-water, as everywhere. Horses. A train car. A '50's Chevy. Bodies, perhaps, and their associated ghost stories.

Stay by me, she says to Dog, stern warning. Be careful.

He heels to her side, attentive.

They look over the drop.

Far below, fish yank bugs from the surface, pull them under in funnels. A willow at the left side of the water's edge trails long arms in the surface. A fallen birch to the right, submerged, makes Sedna bones.

In Manhattan, some time back, the world around her hidden by concrete, she'd walked thirty blocks of Ninth Avenue back to her friend's apartment after a day with the man she loved and could not have—or at least, that was the narrative that had gripped her at the time: on some level, she knew there was both more and less to it than that, that life-preserver-stories come in all shapes and sizes, this one just happened to be a married man. A glorious one, but no less illusory for that.

She had dreamt, upon returning to the apartment in Hell's Kitchen, that she was walking miles of underpasses papered with posters. They advertised something urgent in a language she could not comprehend: no matter how hard she puzzled over them, they made no sense to her, with their garish colors and bold text, dripping fonts and desperate humans bulging and straining from the fading paper glued to cement.

The end of the world was coming, she knew, any second now, and so she tried hard to parse the meaning: nothing, in all this noise. Nothing but the noise itself, cacophonous and lacking all substance. There was nothing green or animal that wasn't poisoned here, and then the world ended.

It was a nuclear flash, she recognized in the meta of the dream: nothing else that blinding, that white. And then the blast. It hurled her forward with incomprehensible speed and power, into the poster-covered wall.

With a sound like a tree branch snapping in a March storm, her spine broke, deep and low.

She died.

And then, she was dancing.

In air that was also water, with a person in a tuxedo who was also a dog, and another dog, and cats, and other people, dead ones, all dead.

She waltzed with this tuxedo-wearing every-dead-beloved (grandfather, best friend burned to death at fourteen, children, familiars, lovers) in the water-air, her hair streaming around her head and her snapped spine irrelevant.

She was completely happy, once she figured out where she was. Cecily retreats from the ledge, wraps her arms around Dog. He smells of flowers.

The scent of gardenia gives you away, my angel, she says. Gabriel García Márquez gave you away.

Dog purrs, deep in his throat. Ripples his skin with pleasure.

Love you so, Angel, she says.

He loves her back.

She finds a stick, hurls it down the trail that leads to the water.

Go swim! She shouts, and behind them, in the clearing, the turkeys rise in an explosion of wings.

I'll meet you down there—

Dog races down the steep path after the stick, all focused intent, his life a shine so bright it illuminates the universe.

She returns to the ledge, green and black depths below.

She thinks she can still fly.

It might break her back, but she's going to do it anyway.

The Inugami Mochi

Dog sits halfway up the steep stair cut into the mountain. The earth's been chopped out, split logs lain in the incisions; winding switchbacks jag sharply up the incline. He's got his Anubis face on; inscrutable and majestic. Brows prominent. Muscles ripple his onyx fur, emphasize his formal posture.

Waiting.

Coming, Dog, Cecily puffs. What can I say, bipedalism sucks.

He watches her foot-placement, impassivity giving way to concern when she has to pull herself up a ridiculously deep step with her hands. His ears arch forward, fall along his muzzle as he gazes down at her scrambling.

Freakin' tall people, she mutters.

Dog sees her carefully to the place where the incline eases and the footholds come closer together again, then rises, trots ahead. Soon the log stair gives way to ground, the incline reverses direction.

It's all rises and falls, getting to the mountain lake—only a half-mile from the pullout on the pass as the crow flies, but it takes twenty five minutes of calf-burning climbs both there and back. Hard going in every direction, Cecily appreciates, except when she's doing it.

Winter wind and ice have shorn the treetops clean off; it's early spring now, and not blowing, so blackflies and deerflies take pint after pint. Peregrines sail. Ravens harass and bark. The occasional moose leaves heaps of pellets the size of tennis balls and giant, cloven hoof-prints on the trail. Elaborate leaf-impressions in the mud match them in size: moose-maple, fecund and striped. Lake Pleiad, hidden in a dip amidst the high swells, is always cold.

On the trail, an unhappily married couple. Cecily can tell by the tension that hangs between them, by the way the man looks at her, the way the woman looks at him looking at her, the combined air of maudlin longing and rage they generate.

As Cecily approaches, he stops, blocking the trail. Asks: "Heading to Lake Pleiad?" His wife, who had been walking faster since she saw Cecily approaching, bumps into his back, rolls her eyes. Cecily nods, appraises the trail edge for a quick way around the couple, can't find one that isn't an obvious brush-off; she skirts them anyway, ducking moose-maple saplings. She meets the woman's gaze as she passes her, nods again. "Have a nice walk," she says. The woman doesn't answer. Her lips are compressed to a thin line. The man says, to Cecily's back: "That's a nice-looking dog you've got there," tries to pat him on his way by.

Dog ducks his hand.

Cecily considers divorce.

Off-mountain, Cecily has been making an effort to 'build community.' Her internet connection and the writing community generated by her blog make it too easy for her live in complete isolation. She'd checked the paper for local events, selected a few where she might find like-minded sorts, started driving down the switchbacks and attending things on the regular, now that the roads weren't ice. She couldn't say it was going well, or involved one-tenth the pleasure of mountain hikes with Dog, but she was following instructions.

At the Progressive Women's Dinner, someone said: "Cecily, why don't you go out with Abigail, since you're at least half-queer? She's single."

"Abigail has the intellect of a bag of hammers," Cecily answered. "My sexual preference is wit."

The women laughed nervously. The bird-like one, whose name Cecily could never retain though she'd met her at least three times now, screeched: "She's not dumb; she's just a very feelings-driven person. She's focused on the spiritual and emotional life more than the life of the mind."

"And homeopathy," Cecily had noted. "And urban legends too stupid to even need debunking. She's pretty focused on those, too."

"I thought we were all Lesbians here," another woman interjected.

Cecily replied: "The all-Lesbian memo apparently didn't go out to the half-queers." An uncomfortable silence fell. Cecily sighed. "Sorry," she said. "I meant for that to be funny."

The women changed the subject to kale, and the evils of butter. Cecily ground her teeth. Craved meat. The company of carnivores. She wondered what Dog was doing at home; if his Kong still had any freeze-dried chicken liver in it, or if he knocked it all loose on the stone floor and ate it in the first three minutes she was gone.

She made an effort. Ruthlessly suppressed all inclinations toward humor, or sarcasm. Assumed an earnest posture. It made her back hurt, but everyone relaxed. She asked people questions about themselves, listened, praised their priorities and concerns, most of which were puzzling to her. As they finished dessert and divvied up the bill, arguing predictably about the tip and who drank what, one of the women, leaning in too close to Cecily, asked if she was going to the bar with them. Cecily demurred, pleading Dog's need to go out.

"I swear that dog is your fucking BOYFRIEND," the woman said.

"No, he's really not," Cecily answered, hackles rising.

"Well, he's keeping you from getting a girlfriend, anyway, so what is he, then?"

The bridge-burning had been building all night.

She paused long enough to consider how she was going to explain this later, decided she didn't care, and said: "What keeps me from choosing a partner of any sex is not meeting many people who aren't petty, dull, jealous, spiteful, competitive, dishonest, bigoted, uncritical, stupid sheep." The woman glared, and Cecily bared a giant grin, all carnivorous teeth. She held it until the woman looked away.

At the door, on the way out, the dinner organizer—who had been in the bathroom during the bridge-burn—wrapped Cecily's arm in hers in a maudlin haze of red wine and said: "It's so important to have real, safe, inclusive community, don't you think?" Cecily started laughing, had trouble stopping. Nervous tension, she supposed.

"I wouldn't know," she said when she caught her breath. "In my experience, there's no such thing."

The organizer looked like she'd been slapped. Cecily sighed again. "Sorry," she said, genuinely so this time. "I'm just— uh—a very truths-driven person."

It's a kind of a disability, the combination of not being willing to lie and having heightened awareness of when other people are doing it. The averted glance, the slight turn, the shoulder stiffening, the tightened grip: the body in motion is a text Cecily speed-reads. She can't not do it; it's innate. It makes her cynical. Dog reads this way, too. It makes him smart. The two of them avoid a lot of trouble because of it, but Cecily tends to land in some as a result, too. She tells Dog about the dinner debacle. He listens to her for a while, then gets bored and goes to the door.

Yeah, yeah, Cecily says. Sometimes you do act like a boyfriend. You've got the attention span of one, anyhow.

Dog raises an eyebrow. Cecily laughs.

They go outside for a moonlight stroll.

They see a barred owl.

Hear coyotes.

Find a luck-stone, quartz band lit by stars.

Walk for miles, Milky Way drunk and silent. Perfectly content.

The next day, she calls her grad-school buddy, with whom she's been making deals about building community and taking purposeful action to reduce her isolation in this very-rural corner of Vermont. "I really don't think I'm a mean person," Cecily says. "I just—I have no tolerance for incongruence between what people say and what they do."

"That describes basically everyone," her friend points out.

"You aren't that way," Cecily says. "You are exactly and precisely what you say you are. I think I'm that way, too. I can have total confidence that you will respond rationally and appropriately to interactions, in total congruence with your stated values and ethics. Why is that asking so much? Animals do that."

"Forebrains are not always helpful," her friend agrees. "They do contribute to and justify very peculiar social behavior."

"Maybe you and I just have Asperger's," Cecily says.

Her friend finds this hilarious and unlikely.

Cecily finds it to be, too, but insists it could be a pretty good explanation. "We're disablingly smart in not-terribly-helpful ways, we find human behavior peculiar and often distasteful—it's that or having been born into the wrong species," she says.

"I suspect that latter explanation is the one more likely to go undiagnosed in this day and age," her friend notes.

"True," Cecily agrees.

Dog discovers the body of Lake Pleiad like it's newly formed for him, every time: the white and gold birch-screen at water's edge gives way and he plows right in at a gallop. A Golden Retriever splashes about in the deep, biting at the spray generated by his own front feet slapping the surface. Dog hurls himself onto the meniscus, crashes through.

Be careful, Cecily says. Even Greg Louganis hits the board sometimes.

Dog ignores her and speeds like a seal, sleek and shining, through the wet to once again hurl himself from shore and crash.

The Golden's human wanders closer to Cecily, says: "They're our babies, aren't they?"

Ducking the question, Cecily says: "What a nice day."

The woman isn't so easily redirected. "It's like the kiddy pool up here."

"I don't have a kid, I have a dog," Cecily says, sharp. "On purpose."

"People do say they replace children for a lot of us," the stranger says, smiling. The "us" abrades Cecily. She never knows what it signifies, except that it's a fiction she usually didn't consent to.

"They've got nothing to do with human children," she snaps. "That diminishes them, and our relationships with them. And in my experience, any pop psychology that presupposes an 'us'—whether it's about women or any other group of individual and disparate beings—is lying from the start."

"How do you see our relationship with dogs, then?" The woman asks the question neutrally, nothing but curiosity in her voice and body.

Cecily realizes she's being a complete asshole, and not holding up her agreement with her grad-school friend to be more welcoming to people, more open to the possibility that they are potential social network, or even, heaven forfend, human friends. This woman might well be creepy or idiotic, or bipedal sandpaper of the emotional variety, but she might also simply be doglike, sniffing and interacting, wagging her tail and making unthreatening displays. Most likely, Cecily decides, she's just still twitchy from the Progressive Women's Dinner.

She walks it back: "Sorry. The subject's just sort of a peeve of mine. I apologize for being rude to you."

The woman shrugs. "You weren't rude. I want to know what you think."

"Why?"

"Beats talking about what a nice day it is, doesn't it?" The woman smiles again.

Cecily decides the woman is just very Golden Retriever, and unlikely to give up on boisterous and largely indiscriminate social interaction, so she smiles back.

"I guess I don't know about anyone else's relationship with dogs, but mine—I usually call him compadre. Or 'Friend.' You know, sort of capitalized in my head. Or my familiar."

"Like from witchcraft?"

"From a lot of places. Every culture has some version of the animal spirit deeply associated with a human, and different language for it." She decides this sounds pedantic, even though it's right, so she appends a question, because this is what people do to make a recognizable and non-threatening opening. "Don't they?"

"I guess they do," the woman says. "Totems." She squats down and picks up a small piece of driftwood, which she then begins to carve with a knife from her belt.

"Yes," Cecily answers, noticing the woman's muscular back, her thick, red hair. "The witch's cat, the kitsune, the kelpie, guardians, meddlers, whatever. It's part of sacred tradition all over the world, in every time." The red-haired woman nods, keeps carving. Cecily can't see what she's making, but decides she likes the shape of the woman's body, the way she smells open, like a moss-covered log in hot sun. She says softly: "In some Japanese traditions, there's the *inugami*. He looks like a dog, but he's a guardian spirit. He's profoundly bonded with his *mochi*—his human—but with a completely independent and unpredictable will of his own. They make each other more powerful than they would be otherwise, and care for one another with deep mutual respect and intimacy. It's not like a human relationship, though. It's something of its own."

"That's lovely," the woman says.

"Yes," Cecily answers. "But in a solemn way. It has risk and costs, too. It's isolating. It has always and everywhere freaked people out, even when they worship it."

"I don't see why."

Cecily has actually thought a lot about why that is, but has never tried to articulate it aloud before. "Maybe because that kind of relationship is by nature exclusionary of the idea that human groups have primacy. Most people are herd animals. The *inugami mochi* has left the group. She and her familiar have a joined experience of the world; one no outside person can share. She has a unique vantage point that is no longer entirely human, and is both honored and feared because of it. Most often feared."

"Burned at the stake."

"Yeah. Or they kill her familiar, because it's the worst thing they can do to her. They tear out half her soul and she never stops bleeding."

"God," the woman says. "I can't imagine."

"Good," Cecily says.

Dog comes by, shakes cold water on Cecily, laughs with crinkled ears, plunges back into the lake. The Golden, a clump of sodden oak leaves stuck on his head, has settled into doing laps: smooth, decorous strokes that don't break the surface, an old lady in an Esther Williams bathing cap. Blissed out.

"I think I had that once," the woman says after they watch the dogs a while. "When I was a child. There was a cat.

I dreamed I was in her, for her whole life. I could see the night fields through her eyes when she hunted. Taste the mouse-blood."

"Yes," Cecily says, surprised. "Like that."

"She disappeared one day. Just didn't come home. Some part of me has never stopped waiting for her. I still have those dreams sometimes. I always wake up sad."

"Yes," Cecily says. "Like that."

The woman rises, extends her hand to Cecily. In it, a small, simple carving of Dog, his joy in water captured in quick edges and sharp spray.

"Take this," the woman says. "A present."

"Holy shit, that's beautiful," Cecily says. She examines it from every angle, deeply impressed by its vividness. "Come home with me," she proposes, without really having intended to, and there is an extremely embarrassing pause, during which Cecily studies the carving and the woman studies her feet.

"Sorry, god, I can't believe I said that," Cecily says eventually. "It's been a long winter."

"I don't really, uh, go that way, usually, I don't think," the woman answers.

Still mortified, but aware of the syntax's implications and noting fluster in peripheral vision, Cecily waits. Looks away. Lets the woman study her.

After a bit, the woman whistles for her Golden, who galumphs out of the water, panting and giggling, all trace of old lady gone. "This is Effluvium," she says. Cecily laughs aloud at the name. "He's not my familiar, but he's funny as hell and I love him."

Cecily rubs the wet dog, who leans on her passionately, wiggling and smelling of rotten vegetables. "He's been in the swampy part," she notes.

"Yeah," the woman says. "Haven't we all. Can he come home with you, too?"

"'Course," Cecily answers. "I have freeze-dried liver. And dehydrated sweet potatoes."

Look at this, Cecily says to Dog later, after the woman and Effluvium have gone, holding out the carving from Lake Pleiad. It's you. Really you. She nailed it.

Dog noses it gently, curls his nose under his tail and sleeps.

I like that she didn't tell me her name, and that it didn't occur to me to ask, Cecily says.

She imagines that later, a month or three on, she'll bump into the woman in the co-op, or at the hardware store, and it will be terribly awkward: to fill the scarlet silence, she'll introduce herself to the husband, who will sense the awkwardness but not be able to put a finger on it. The woman will tell him some small and easy lie on the way home, and life will go on.

For now, she likes that her sheets and her face smell like mossy logs in hot sun. She won't wash either until she really has to.

Back on the trail to Lake Pleiad, Cecily huffs down the last incline to the water. Dog has bounded ahead, all stiff-legged rocking-horse gait as reserved for particularly joyous green-gold-blue days.

He tears into the water after the stick she throws, brings it back in a glitter of spray. She throws it again. Seventy miles an hour, his glorious water entry, she thinks, and he retrieves it, his iridescent black fur blue in all this brilliant light. A third time, galloping like Poseidon's steeds—and then Dog screams.

He's in an unnatural position in the water: vertical and writhing.

He is screaming.

It is the worst sound she has ever heard.

She sprints into the water after him, up to her shoulders: he's stuck in something, oh god oh fuck, he's impaled on something: a huge limb of a tree has fallen into the lake, entirely invisible from the shore, and he's impaled on a branch the thickness of her wrist. It's sunk into his abdomen, and he's screaming. Her stoic Dog, who hides pain always: he's screaming and screaming a soul-destroying scream and she can't walk it back, she can't make this not be happening.

Everything takes on the hyper-clarity of life and death, of what must be done. Adrenaline floods her body.

In an EMT class ages past, she learned that whenever possible, before moving the patient, one should saw off the impaling object without moving it in the wound, so they don't bleed out when it's pulled.

Up to her shoulders in the remote mountain lake, Dog screaming in terrified agony, the tree under the waves massive, she does what must be done: she wraps her arms low around Dog's screaming body, feels for the impaling branch, ducks under water and braces her feet against the fallen trunk, gets the angle as right as she can, and yanks him off it with all the power in her. His yipping scream goes south, to horror-pain, echoing across miles. She holds the hole in him shut, flails to shore, puts his legs on the ground. They do not hold. Her hands and arms are covered with blood.

Oh god, oh Dog, hold on, okay, I have you, I have you beloved, okay, we're going to be okay, oh god, oh Dog, you're okay,

I have you comes out of her in a steady stream as people from the far side of the lake begin to drift slowly toward her and she takes that in, discards them as useless to her and Dog, examines the hole in him as best as she can: it's full of tree-shards and mud, it's pouring blood, she can see too much glistening in there, she can't tell if it's intestine or muscle, she hopes it's muscle, there is no cell signal on this mountain, it's a forty-five minute drive down to the vet in town, it's Saturday, it will be past three when they can possibly get there, they close at three on Saturdays, there's an answering service, she'll break down the fucking door if she has to, and as she's thinking all this, she's pulling the wound-edges together and gripping them in a tight fist slick with blood, Dog's legs have gone entirely rubber, he weighs seventy-seven pounds, she knows this because he just had a check-up during which his beefcake muscle and glow of health from all this mountaineering was much admired, her spinal injury means she can't much lift over forty pounds at a whack without collapse of her own, so it's going to have to be adrenaline, then—and she lifts him in her arms, still holding him shut where his life is spilling out, and she settles him into as good a grip as she can get, and she starts to run.

And she runs. And runs.

Up the steep trail, holding him, trying not to bounce him, the steady patter of *we're okay, Dog, you're okay, I have you, just a little further, okay my love, you're okay, hang on beloved, we're going to be okay* falling out of her as fast as his blood is falling out of him, making it harder and harder to grip the slick flesh closed, even his fur becoming slick, a seal in her arms, slippery and huge, so heavy, and the word *deadweight* comes into her head and she banishes it and runs faster, the patter falling from her mouth louder now, from panic and burning lungs thudding up and down the ski-trails and passes and switchbacks leading back to the road, and when they come to the steep stair cut into the mountain face, the one with logs laid as steps five, six feet apart and steep as fuck, the one where he always watched over her climb to be sure she didn't fall on her ass while she complained about tall people, she knows she's in trouble, and she can't think how she's going to get him up that, and he cries in her arms, and she has to put him down, and she has to stay low over him to hold the hole in him closed, and she has to say the worst thing she has ever said in her life, holding in his guts in her blood-slick hands: *Dog, I'm so sorry, I have to ask you to help me now, I can't get you up this by myself, can you help me? Oh god, Dog, I'm so sorry. I need you to try, okay, Dog? I need you to do this, there is no other way, I need you to live through this, Dog, do you understand me? I'm so sorry, my Dog-god, my love, oh god, we have to get up this thing, we have to try, okay? You have to help me now, I'm so sorry—*

And Dog looks at her with pain-clouds in his eyes and hyperventilating pant and flinching lips exposing his beautiful white teeth and says: *yes, Cecily, I will try,* and her heart breaks into a million shards on the rocks.

She lifts him one steep increment at a time, propping him on his own wobbling legs and holding him shut as best as she can, and he stiffens as best as he can, and he pulls himself up by his front paws, claws sunk into log-steps, muscles shaking, and now Cecily is crying, and crying, and lifting, and holding him shut, and scraping them both up the impossible section, and then they are past it and she gathers him in again and holds his wound shut and again begins to run, close to the road now, a final series of hills, her arms and legs and lungs and spine flaming, his weight somehow more dense now even than it was, and the denseness terrifies her, and sends new surges of adrenaline that get them to the car, where she fumbles him into the passenger seat, propped, and she flies to the driver's side, and when she gets in, she sees that his gums, exposed by his grimacing pant, are white as snow, and she screams at him *don't you fucking die on me Dog don't you do it we're almost there okay you're okay you're going to be okay we're okay we're almost there YOU ARE NOT ALLOWED TO DIE* and she sends the car hurtling down the switchbacks, her right hand leaving his wound only to shift, blood spattering the windshield with every flick back and forth, she lets it hurtle in neutral down the steep grades while she holds him together, a barely controlled fall down the mountain at insane and deathly speeds, and in twenty minutes, they're in cell-tower range, and she's called the answering service for the vet, and they are stupid and incompetent, and she calls again and again until they vow the vet is on his way, and in thirty minutes she's in the vet's parking lot, and it's almost four, and no one's there to meet her, and she leaves Dog in the passenger seat saying *I will be right back, I will be right back, you hold on my love, I will be right back* and she runs across the street to the first house and bangs on the door and no one answers and so she runs to the second house and bangs and bangs and yells until someone in boxers and nothing else appears, and she rants and raves about ice and he gives her a tray of cubes from his freezer and a dishcloth and she sprints back to the car and yanks open the door and Dog's eyes are clouded and vague and his tongue is white now, too, and she screams at him *you hold on, my angel, you HOLD ON*, and she packs the wound with the ice and he doesn't even flinch, his head lolls onto her shoulder and she wails *beloved, my beloved, my beloved hold on* and they are like this for what seems a very long time before the vet comes careening into the parking lot and pushes Cecily out of the way and carries Dog in his arms like a bride across the threshold of the office.

In moments like this, everything goes both very fast and very slow. The vet has one of those tables that rises and lowers:

he puts Dog on his feet on the table at floor-height, and Dog falls. The vet turns him on his side, jacks the table up, pulls in a strong, brilliant light and examines the wound for a long, long, silent time. He listens to Dog's heart and lungs. He presses Dog's gums and tongue, and his lips go thin when nothing much happens to the pale, pale flesh.

He turns and looks at Cecily: she is blood-covered, shaking, afire, silent, urgent, staring him into the next world, or bridging to him from it with her flaming gaze, across the divide, Dog's life in their hands.

"You have to save him," she whispers. "Save us."

He stares back. Opens his mouth to speak, closes it again. Thinks.

"Here's how it is," he says at last. "The ice was smart. It closed things up a bit. Probably helped the pain. There's a lot of mess in there. Tearing. Detritus. A high risk of infection. Without cutting, I can't tell if it perforated his intestinal wall—or if it did, how much damage there is. He's hanging on hard, but he's in shock, and he may or may not make it. I am here by myself. I can try to do this. I might succeed. But I have no staff, no backup. I believe he is stable enough right now to make it to the Burlington Emergency Veterinary Hospital. They are excellent surgeons. I know them, and I know they can do better than I can. But it's a risk. If you go, I can't give him anything at all for pain, because they need to decide what anesthesia to use. You'd have to get there fast."

Cecily shudders. The silence stretches. Five seconds. Ten. An elongated fifteen seconds, equivalent to years.

"Tell me what to do," she cries out, finally. "I don't know which risk to take. He is everything. He is everything. I can't make the wrong choice. Oh god, Dog, tell me what to do—" and to the vet again: "Which do I do?"

"Go," he says. "Go now. Drive like hell. I'm calling them as soon as you're out the door. They'll be ready for him." He lifts Dog off the table, deposits him in Cecily's arms. "GO."

She runs.

Hurtling up Route Seven, into the city. Forty minutes. Dog lolls sideways against the window, his tongue caught between his own teeth now. Her hand on his ribs, pleading with him the whole way, a steady rain of calling, calling, calling him, *don't leave, Dog, oh god, Dog, stay, stay with me, I have you, I have you beloved.*

BEVS blessedly close to the highway.

A tech runs out to her in the entryway, gathers Dog from her arms, weighs him—yes, seventy seven pounds—for anesthesia. Says to Cecily: "We have to triage, there's one other in worse shape, believe it or not, come with me," and she puts Cecily and Dog together in a huge cage on the floor, on sheepskins. The vet races by and shoots him up with some canine narcotic, says to Cecily: "This is basically heroin, he might nod and puke, you just hold him, and hold this pan under his head, and talk to him, try to keep him calm, not moving," and they give her a pan, and she holds him, and holds the pan under his head, and he nods and drools copiously but doesn't puke, and she whispers love to him in every language they know, she sings him Sam Cooke's "Cupid," their love-song, her voice does not shake, she strokes his elaborate ears, extra-fancy, she calls them as always, and when they stabilize the Saint Bernard who wasn't breathing, they come for Dog, and put him on the surgical table, and have Cecily hold his head while they intubate him and wrap his muzzle in gauze, and she whispers *love, love,* and says *I have you, beloved, I'm right here, I have you, we're okay, you're going to make it, I'm right here, you come back and find me right here in a little while after they help you, you're okay my love, we're okay,* and they put a mask over his nose, and his eyes roll back into his head and then he is unconscious.

The moment he goes out, Cecily starts to shake at the depth of bone, from her feet to the top of her head, and tears fly out of her eyes. She ripples in the air itself, white as paper, wobbling.

The surgeon does a double-take at the sudden collapse of what had until then been a hyper-functional being who was clearly good in a crisis, and says: "Are you okay? Look, whether you are or aren't, you need to go outside now, don't puke here, I need to save him," and Cecily backs up a few steps, and sees the scalpels come out, and a nurse shoves her out the door, and she runs for the parking lot and gets out there just in time for the puke to hit pavement.

She sits on the curb in the parking lot, sobbing, shaking, in post-adrenaline-flood sickness, and chants under her breath: Dog-god, Dog-god, beloved, come back to me.

Time ticks by. City bats come out, disappear into dusk.

She goes in, they shake their heads to indicate *no news, not finished yet*; she goes back out.

It is dark blue and lilac-scented in the parking lot. Stars came out, move long distances.

She goes in, they shake their heads to indicate *no news, not finished yet*; she goes back out.

It is black and a copper-tasting wind off Champlain bathes the parking lot. Orion. Ursa Major. The Pleiades. The fucking Pleiades.

She goes in, they shake their heads to indicate *no news, not finished yet*; she goes back out.

She calls her friend in California who was supposed to be coming out to Vermont for two weeks in a few days, to see if they would be a family, her and him and Dog, after years of epistolary relationship that could be love but could also be weird: they'd never met in person, and were also best friends.

He answers on the first ring, something glib and funny as he always did when she called. She gets out his name, bursts into hysterical sobs again, unintelligible.

"Cecily, what's happened?"

She manages: "Dog," and nothing else for several minutes, hitching and coughing with tears. "He's in surgery, he's been in there for hours—he might not make it—impaled—I got him down off the mountain, but he might not make it—" and her friend gathers bits and pieces of the story, asks sensible questions she can't make sense of, has her walk the cell phone into the reception area and hand the phone to the person working there, gives them his credit card number and fronts the $1,200.00 they require, gets Cecily back on the phone, tells her to worry about that later when she knows where she is and where her wallet is and what is needed and what is going to be needed when Dog is awake and stable, which he will be any time now, he says: "Any time now, he's going to be awake and stable, any time now," crooning. "You're okay, you and Dog, you're okay, I'm here with you, you're going to be okay, both of you, he's coming back to you, Cecily, you and Dog are an epic with many verses to go, what you've both been through today is unspeakable but he has you, he'll make it, he's coming back."

After some time, Cecily is composed enough to say: "No matter what else ever happens or doesn't between us, I will never, ever forget what you did for me tonight."

"Don't even," he answers.

"Oh god," Cecily says. "I see the surgeon. She's coming out. She's nodding."

"Go," her friend says. "Go. Call me back when you can." And hangs up.

By the time Cecily got Dog back home, it was almost dawn, light streaking the edges of the sky pale. Somewhere in the course of the night, the adrenaline supply had run out entirely, remains puked up and nothing left to hide the catastrophic failure of her already-damaged spine, which was now somehow both locked and liquid, unbending and unhinged from all pelvic moorings.

Dog was semi-conscious in the back of the car, and she couldn't lift him out.

Finally, she got down on the ground on her knees beside the foot-well and pulled him from the bench seat onto her body, cradled in her lap.

She was unable to rise. She tried, tried again, kept trying—and could not.

She shuffled, on her knees, his body in her arms, to the door. Opened it. Slid them through. Closed it. Pulled herself up, leaving him on the carpet. Made a bed of layers of blankets on the living room floor, knowing stairs were out of the question. Piled towels where Dog would sleep, to absorb the pink-tinged fluid leaking from the drainage tube inserted behind rows of surgical staples covering his shaved belly like shining teeth. Pulled them both onto the makeshift nest. Wrapped herself carefully around him, spooning his back, breathing his ruff. Both of them still caked with blood and lake-mud and drags of green and drool and puke. They slept.

They'd sent him home: she lived far enough away that it would be hard to come and go, they knew and trusted her local vet to do the follow-up, and he'd told them Cecily could handle the daily care.

The daily care involved drugs that kept him reasonably vague about the pain, well dosed with antibiotics, stool-softened, anti-inflamed.

Helping him navigate his way outside to pee, which he did leaning forward in a sort of cautious, adapted puppy-squat, and poop, which didn't happen at all for a while, until he figured out how to manage the muscles and position in a way that could work, torn and sewn and stapled as he was.

It also involved soaking the drain in water so hot it was just barely tolerable on his incision, every few hours. Over and over and over, every day.

Dog let Cecily do all this without complaint, even about the searing pain of the soakings. She murmured and crooned, she told him how brave and strong he was. She thanked him, again and again, for being so strong and brave, for coming back to her, for staying. He gazed at her with mildly embarrassed eyes, apologetic for being so fucked up and broken, clear that every time she touched him, no matter how much it hurt, it was to rebuild his body with love.

She poured her consciousness into his flesh.

This vein. This muscle. This nerve. Come back. Live.

The tree branch, it turned out, had missed his femoral artery by a quarter of an inch. Had it not, he would have bled out right on shore, in a minute or three. The capillaries through his abdomen and thigh were ripped apart and he lost too much, but he did not bleed to death.

It entered inguinally, pointed back toward his tail: his abdominal muscles were shredded, and full of tree that took many hours to remove, but it did not perforate his intestine. By another slim fraction of an inch, his beautiful muscle had held, and protected his guts. Torn to a million ripped-up strands, but it held.

There was no sepsis.

Under the staples, the drain that hung out on either side.

Under the drain: a layer-cake of stitched-together muscle, reconstructed.

Under the layers of rebuilt abdominal wall: his life.

Intact.

A steep trail to climb, the recovery he was facing.

Cecily too, re-injured as she was, and worse than before, unable to bend, pain ripping through her always now.

But alive, and the Us of them, intact.

Three days after she brought him home, she was confident enough in his stability to leave the room for a few minutes while he slept, drugged and deep. She went upstairs and checked her email: it was full of PayPal notifications. Puzzled, thinking it must be a mistake, she flipped to her blog.

Her California friend had posted on his own, linking in to hers so it showed on her dashboard:

Dog's been badly hurt. It looks like he's going to be okay, but it's going to cost a fortune. Those of you who read Cecily's blog already know and love Dog from his appearances there. Or you love her. Listen, if you can and are so inspired, now would be a good time to put something in her tip jar, to help with vet bills. It's a steep road they're on.

There was almost a thousand dollars in her PayPal account, entirely from people who only knew Dog virtually, from her writing about their adventures over the last several years. Each donation came with a note:

Get well, Dog.

Be strong, Dog.

Hang in there, Cecily.

We love you, Dog.

The love story between Cecily and Dog is an extraordinary epic I feel honored to be a part of – sending strength to both of you.

You can do this, Dog & Cecily.

Oh, Dog—you get better, we need you!

You two have shown me what's possible in this world, in love, between human and animal, in all things. I wish I could do more to help repay all I've learned from you.

Please, please recover, Dog. Please, please take care, Cecily.

Love, love, love to beautiful Dog and his human beloved.

Cecily cried.

She cried and cried and cried. Sometimes her own species redeemed itself so spectacularly it made rubble of her heart.

Many years later, after Dog was dead, Cecily explained to her California friend what happened during his visit to Vermont: that eighty percent of her was absent, deeply inside Dog's body, knitting together his muscles, sealing leaking capillaries, re-building broken nerve connections by sheer effort of mind-will, her soul swimming the summery streets of his veins, as Roethke called them, with a needle and thread in her teeth, stopping to mend, mend, mend anywhere she saw anything out of place.

"I didn't have much attention to spare," she said, "and you needed so much. I was giving him everything I had."

This was true.

What was also true: even in the airport, she'd known.

She could smell on his neck the incongruence: read in the movement of his body the vast chasms she couldn't possibly fill and didn't want to. It made her so sad.

"There has never been a day," she said, "and there won't be, when I haven't been grateful to you for how you helped us in those weeks. On the phone with me at BEVS. Driving us both to physical therapy. The picnic in the field of daisies, blanket littered with our broken bodies. Just being there. Knowing what it meant."

"His chin on my shoulder in the car," her friend said. "I'll never forget that he gave me that."

Many years later, after Dog was dead, this worst day of her life became something else for Cecily.

Not just the second-worst day.

A blue-gold-green day of stiff-legged rocking-horse gait, because he lived. He was alive that day. All the way through all of the horror, he was alive. And that made it a joyous day.

Vibrant and whole.

In Vermont, Cecily knelt on the floor, Dog standing braced against her hip.

Now stretch, she said, and gently extended his left leg backward, knee straight, toes pointed.

Now bend, she said, and brought Dog's leg back in, knee curled, toes almost touching his scarred belly.

Now stretch, extending.

Now bend, curling in, his iridescent black fur shining, the scent of gardenias rising from his skin.

Over and over. Fifty times. Every day.

By autumn, he'd be running again, and when a stick touched his underside in the woods or water, he would no longer flinch. By the following year, circulation to his foot was fully restored and his leg no longer cramped.

How he swam, glorious Dog.

How valiant, his lifelong love of water. Even after. Especially then.

Now my turn, she said, and did her own physical therapy, Dog lying on the rug beside her while she tried to recruit muscle to do what bone and ligament could not anymore.

His paw on her hand.

Now stretch, he said. Now bend.

Giggling, both of them.

Knitting themselves back together in a pool of golden light.

Copper T

Dog says: come on you're missing something come on you're going to miss it.

He's not referring to anything specific, he's referring to possibility. This is why Cecily needs him.

She'd been standing in the middle of the room again, dish-towel in hand, staring at the floor and trying to think: I just have to think, she'd said, before miring, before Dog stamped his foot at her, went to the door and kicked it. Right, she'd said, and taken him for a long and ginger walk, light-headed green and gold miles, slowly.

She was bleeding a lot. It was making her vague. Or some of the vagueness was the bleeding, anyway.

At one point, a few weeks out, she'd called the doc, appalled by what was still happening in her pants: she'd been instructed to take an iron supplement.

"Okay," she'd said, "I will, but maybe what I really need to do is buy stock in adult diapers? Or better yet, in large plastic buckets, which are now my preferred seating option?" The doc had laughed, said it should improve after a while. "Can you remind me approximately what time is 'a while'?" she'd asked, and again the doc laughed, noting that Cecily was hilarious.

This was the down side of using humor as a coping mechanism, Cecily knew. The up side: she hadn't yet completely flipped out. Or bled to death, so there was still hope.

When she'd been on the table for forty minutes—every attempt to get the IUD through her cervix failing, blood and Betadine splattered across her legs, the instrument table, the floor—the doc had started chanting, soothingly, that her cervix was doing an excellent job, it was doing precisely what it was there to do, which was to keep everyone out of her uterus, and Cecily had shouted through clenched teeth, blood even in her mouth from catching some part of her own flesh between teeth in full brace against pain, "why doesn't it work with Republicans!?" The doc had howled, and stopped what she was doing, patted Cecily's gory knee, and proposed rescheduling and trying again, reminding her that sometimes with women who haven't had children, insertion wasn't that easy because the cervix had never dilated fully, and obviously the dilation drug hadn't quite—

"If I get up off this table right now," Cecily had interrupted, "I am never getting back on it. FINISH IT."

The doc had gotten some new instruments which Cecily carefully didn't look at, imagining chisels and sledgehammers. She'd finished it.

A couple of months later, a man apparently meeting all the criteria of wit invited her to go berrying, which seemed a deeply perfect invitation: it was July in New England. Eight, nine weeks out from the IUD debacle and she was still burning through super-plus tampons in twenty minutes, but she was more functional now, and sometimes the bleeding even stopped entirely for a few days at a time. She ate a protein bar, went berrying. Eventually, with some real optimism, ended up in bed with him.

The triumphal lack of concern about birth control was liberating.

The resulting UTI, and the life-threatening allergic reaction to the antibiotics, not so much.

There had been such a sensible discussion. About a non-hormonal solution to all potential future need for birth control probably seeing Cecily right through to menopause ("These things can stay in there for ten, twelve years!"), about insurance coverage that wouldn't be in place much longer since Cecily's teaching gig had run out but would cover every cent right now, about how it was a ten minute procedure, in-office, a little cramping, maybe somewhat longer and heavier periods but nothing unmanageable, about whether or not Cecily would be fit to perform well in the job interview she had scheduled for the morning following the insertion ("Oh, yeah, you'll take some Ibuprofen, no biggie"), how much safer and better IUD's are now, a great solution.

"I'm not even sexually active right now," Cecily had said.

"You're a hottie," her doc had said. "You will be!"

"That'd be awesome," Cecily had answered. "I'm a picky hottie with bad luck and a dog who makes humans look bad, though, so it's problematic."

About the UTI and antibiotic allergy, the berrying man informed Cecily that the whole sex equals death thing was a bit heavy for him, and split.

Later, shamed by friends, he apologized and made some solicitous noises he made sure did not actually sign him up for anything.

She saw herself through the allergic reaction, Epi-Pen in hand and Benadrylled into a dope-haze Dog found extremely peculiar and mildly amusing, especially when she didn't quite aim properly at doorways and bounced off the doorframe. She did not have to be hospitalized.

"Well," the doc had said, when the insertion was over. Blood was splattered everywhere. A discarded spike of some kind that did not bear close examination was on the floor in a pool of blood. A clamp. Reddened towels. "That wasn't easy."

"You're really lucky I like you," Cecily had mumbled, doubled over and hemorrhaging into a pad the size of Manhattan.

In the parking lot after the insertion, she'd hyperventilated. Made it into the driver's seat of the car. Sat until she stopped shaking. Drove home, concentrating furiously on the painted lines. Passed out.

Later, when she'd cleaned up the mess she'd woken in, she eased back down with Dog, whose ears had been in constant alarm-position since he smelled her bright-copper scent, sensed her dim outline. Curled in a ball, a Ginsu Knives commercial running on a loop in her uterus, she'd whispered to him, triumphant: I'm impregnable.

The next morning, she'd risen at six, gone into the bathroom to shower for her job interview. Blood poured down her legs, through the super-plus tampon, around the saturated maxi pad under it, through underwear and sweatpants and socks, leaving prints on the floor. Then her whole body drenched in an instant, inexplicable sweat that soaked through her sweatshirt and actually dripped off her face, her chest, diluting the river of blood. Everything went gray and spinny, so she'd aimed for the floor: came to on it, having fainted for the first time in her life. She was not a fainting sort of person, but before she could quite grasp what had happened, she was puking her brains out, grateful to have landed so close to the toilet. When there was nothing left, not even bile, she'd risen, shaking. Cleaned the floor, bleached everything. Showered and brushed her teeth, careful not to ingest even a drop of water that might eject itself from her in some way. Put on a suit. Driven to her interview, concentrating hard on the painted lines of the road. Gotten a tight grip on herself outside the building: used breathing techniques to control the shaking, the dizziness. Checked her face: it was somewhere between green and gray, sort of the color of lichen. There was nothing she could do about that.

She was pretty sure she'd been coherent, and maybe even mildly impressive in moments, during the interview. She had not thrown up on the table, or shaken visibly. When she left, she imagined the conversation between the interviewers: "Nice woman, great skills. Funny color, though. And maybe a little vague around the edges?" She'd never heard back from them.

Later, when the doc got back to her, she'd said: "Huh, I don't know. That's weird. People don't usually react to the dilator drug that way. Probably food poisoning or something. Let me know if you keep throwing up. Dehydration's no good."

"I hate you," Cecily had answered.

The berrying man's apparently functional wit didn't hold up well in general, contingent as it was on steady consumption of beer and dope, staying in his house, and somaticizing, in the form of crippling diarrhea, any and all emotional discomfort caused by occasional forced confrontation with the inconvenient reality of other people.

She tried hard, in the interest of all the external measures by which they seemed a great match—editors, writers, teachers, both of them—to rationalize this, to create elaborate systems of explanations in which it made sense, but within a couple of weeks it was clear that the Occam's razor of the situation was that he was probably just an asshole.

Dog had eased himself up and down off the bed gently, without shaking it, for weeks: slept with his back pressed carefully into the curve of Cecily's stomach until she stopped smelling broken and started taking him into the woods again. She had moved carefully. Several times a day, she'd hissed in air suddenly, through clenched teeth, when pain shot through her uterus for no apparent reason, or because her belt pressed across the area when she bent to tie her shoe, or because she had to pee and her bladder exerted some small pressure. The pain-hiss made Dog nervous. He stayed close by her side, solicitous.

At no time was she unaware of the metal passenger in her body: its shape and position, its bright, sharp gleam.

Cecily found herself watching berrying man with increasing amazement on their last date at his house. Stunningly patronizing. Spectacularly arrogant. Dismissive of everyone to a theatrical degree. It was like watching someone perform a badly written part: Cecily had a hard time believing what was actually coming out of his mouth, at times, and reconciling this with the peculiar reality that the sex was really fun. Lying in bed, she wanted to know if he realized he sounded like a dead white guy aspirant, oppressed by expectation that he not be a misogynist. He'd shrugged, poked at her arm. Wanted to know if she'd always been this size, or if, you know—"What," Cecily had asked, not even surprised at this point by the non sequitur. "You want to know if I'm a secret fatty waiting to come out?" She'd been off food entirely for too much of the preceding six months, and was as small as she could get without bone loss; this was a thing that happened with her sometimes, and caused her to be confused with an entirely different kind of person. He'd shrugged. Shown her the porn mag he'd produced some years back, pointed out how clever and funny it was that they'd put the magazine's bar code over the naked, emaciated girl's vulva.

"It's ironic, the placement," he'd said.

"Not so much, actually," she'd answered.

Shortly thereafter, he'd put his foot on Dog's spine and shoved.

"What the fuck do you think you're doing," she'd hissed.

"He was in my way," he'd whined.

"Done," she'd said, and collected Dog's bed from the nook where she'd left it for the times she stayed the night.

She'd cried all the way down the mountainous miles back to her place, without wanting to. Such waste, such ugliness, such loss of control over the quality of their lives, hers and Dog's, the invasion of metaphor implicit in that: she was a river and flood, a faucet and drip.

There wasn't much she could do about it. The cascades of losses in this arena, the unrelenting pointlessness of effort: the almost ridiculous stubbornness of longing for what she always thought should be easy but which never was.

"I think I have Catastrophe-Pussy," she'd told a friend. "All I have to do is take off my pants and something terrible happens."

Her friend had laughed and laughed. Cecily was so funny.

Lichen-green, the lack of optimism. Oxygenated red, the disgust.

He didn't hurt me, Dog had said on the way home, putting his paw over hers on the gearshift as she drove. It's not a big deal.

Yes it is, Cecily had answered.

Cecily decided she would not allow anyone from any medical field of any kind to touch her body for any reason, for the foreseeable future, and swore off dating again. "No touchy, no feely is my new policy," she'd announced to some friends, after regaling them with the whole bloody story from Republicans to Occam's Razor to Catastrophe Pussy. "My homeostasis may not be great, but I know how to manage it, damn it."

They'd laughed and laughed. Cecily was too hilarious.

In 3D as much as on Facebook or by email, she sometimes sensed that she was a symbol, an icon, really. To married men especially. Honore de Balzac's jaguar: "she was white like the sands, tawny like the sands, solitary and burning like the sands." Her aloneness, her hand-crafted writer's life, her peripatetic teaching travels: this looked like freedom to them, reminded them who they were when they were not a we.

The Us of Dog and Cecily was not something they recognized, but there was truth in their vision of her, to a degree: they just softened all the edges, flattened out all the risks and consequences so they could comfortably huddle near this remembrance, attracted.

Mostly, this grossed her out.

She knew she did the same thing, of course: flattened out their lives to noise and chaos and television and shrieking details of the-things-we-are-expected-to-do destroying all rich, alluvial silence and vegetable growth on plains never given a chance to be free of flood.

That was also true, to a degree. They were busy and noisy in human ways the animal in her could not tolerate. Occasionally, though, she looked back at their sleek and complacent not-aloneness, their reliable cars from steady income, the pictures of them with their families, and felt the same longing they did; they represented the road she didn't take, what she gave up to have this other thing.

Cecily watches Masterpiece Theater, with Dog asleep along her leg. His chin on her lap, his paw holding her calf for sleep-anchor; her hand in his ruff, holding on for life.

There is a new declivity at his temple, a vulnerability about his eyes under his white brows. He'd had a seizure a few weeks back: petit mal, and the vet wasn't too concerned, they just made plans for all possibilities, including that it might not happen again.

He is aging, the vet had said. Things will change faster from here.

He is just aging, Cecily hopes, tracing the sucked-in flesh and weeping silently for Dog's mortality, not to wake him. He's so deep he doesn't even feel her touch, unless in dreams.

Since the seizure, he's been sleeping this way. Like the dead.

Cecily prefers her life as it is, almost all the time.

Dog. The forest. Wellsprings of silence and solitude. Dipping in to noise and chaos as necessary. Maintaining her homeostasis, which might not be perfect but is manageable, and inviting others in as seemed worth the risk.

She knows the New Age people have wrecked many worlds theory for everyone else, but sometimes she dwells on those tightly curled other universes; ones where—among so many other yeses—longing doesn't have to remain subtext in careful messages. Always polite. Respectful of boundaries.

"I envy your life," someone writes in a comment on her Facebook feed, when she posts about shifting her editing projects and taking off for a ten mile hike with Dog. "Your freedom."

Below that comment, a picture of a man she likes and respects a lot. He stands in the Nevada desert with his beautiful wife. They're both smiling. Relaxed, easy smiles, resting against one another, easily.

Look, she says to Dog, whose head is on her thigh and whose flag of a tail is waving slowly, to gradually pull her attention away from the computer and into fixing him supper. What a joyous photograph, she says.

It's their hands, though, that undo her: their partly entwined fingers, how they appear to be gently unlacing each other.

THE LAKE HOUSE

DOG AND CECILY COLLIDE in the doorframe. Cecily has stopped suddenly, so Dog waits to see whether this will be one of the times she pushes through, or if she will back up, shut and lock the door, go sit on the couch and stare at the wall. He noses the back of her knee gently; steals glances at her face, grown sharp and pointed.

After a time, she goes forward, slapping her thigh for Dog to come along. In the snow, he puts an encouraging jaunt into his step, spring-coiled and engaging, leaving spirals of track for her to plow through, head down.

It's like he never existed, Cecily says, when they reach the ice-edge. Or like we didn't.

I know, Dog says, putting himself between Cecily and the frozen lake. But look at this stick.

Cecily stares at her feet.

It's beautiful, Dog points out. Cedar, I think. Or maybe just white pine. But nice. Smell it.

I guess we didn't, Cecily breathes. The words hang visible in fierce cold, knives and staffs she could snatch from the air and hurl against tree trunks, shattering ice-encased branches.

Not really. Not real.

Dog stamps his feet. Puffs hot-breath at Cecily's cold hands, limp at her sides.

That's a nice one you have, she notices eventually. Is it cedar? She picks it up, throws it: it hits a slippery patch on the trail, skitters out onto the frozen lake surface.

Dog thunders after it, runs onto the ice.

Cecily shouts, runs after him.

The ice holds them up.

He brings the stick back to her, heat rippling from his body. Heart hammering, she stays close to him, on solid ground. Keeps away from the edge. Doesn't touch any more sticks.

In the morning, she adds untouched rice and beans and chicken to Dog's breakfast. In the evening, she cooks two eggs, gives him one. In the night, she wakes shivering from dreams of her own bones rattling against each other, ice-encased. Her ribs a cruel map of his hands. Dog curls into the backs of her knees, throwing heat. Her pelvic bones, grown pointed and sharp, cut the sheets—or Dog does, turning and digging and nesting beside her: it doesn't matter, she wants to throw away all the sheets anyway. They abrade. It hurts. She writes it all down. Images repeat, bleed from one piece into the next. Somewhere in the dark, there should be something hot and soft, something not-jagged, un-sharp: something that lets her rest. She can't find it. She thrashes in her sleep, violently. Dog presses against her back. Whines. It's like she's trying to reach the surface but her limbs are frozen. Slower and slower, liquid to solid. Dog kicks her, hard. Puts his head on her hip. She settles.

Morning comes.

She cooks two eggs. Stares at them. Gives them to Dog.

In the walls of the lake house she has rented, there are squirrels. Usually, squirrels aren't a problem, but this particular horde is as destructive as they are raucous: they eat the joists, make her room smell like a nest, play acorn-hockey all night, piss and argue day in and day out.

She doesn't want to call the landlord. When he comes, he doesn't leave; he finds excuses to come back again and again, for weeks, asking personal questions and standing too close until only extreme rudeness makes him go away again. He's the type to lay poison, in spite of Dog. She can't have that. Besides, then there would just be corpses in the walls, rotting, slowly. Months, the smell of death. Or he'd tear out her ceilings, upend her life for weeks and lurk about the place day in and day out, noisy and invasive, pissing in corners. She'd rather deal with the squirrels.

She tries to find their access routes so she can lay Hav-A-Hart traps or build those smart one-way gates to lock them out. She searches the perimeter for the place they get in: under the deck. Under the eaves. Behind the gingerbread detail above the balcony. Through some torn piece of flashing. She can't find the door. They are the last and first thing she hears every day, come in to escape the cold. Her bedroom used to be so quiet.

She asks the man she's just started dating for his help: he's glad to try, but even with his ladders and her flashlights, their combined experience with rural hazards, they can't find any sign of where the criminal rodents are getting in and getting out. Baffled, they resort to coffee, standing too close and staring up at the pristine flashing, gap-free. They speculate about underground highways under the brick patio, over- and under-passes, rotaries, on and off ramps. They laugh, and Cecily knows she'll probably have sex with him this visit. She can smell that he's bi-polar, largely untreated: a dry, hot smell like flint-sparks. She's decided that all contexts considered, it probably doesn't matter. They might be able to ease each other's way a bit. For a while. Until he blows. It might help her eat. He's lonely, too, and also doesn't eat enough.

He says he just wants to look under the deck one more time. Seems the likeliest spot they might have missed.

"Sure," Cecily says. "Then I'll cook us something."

Dog is unhelpful, having long-since decided to ignore the problem of squirrels. When he was a puppy, in a different country house with similar issues, Cecily used to shout CRIMINALS! and point to the ceiling: he'd jump onto the bed and bark his head off at them until she collapsed with laughter at the sound of their criminal little rodent feet scattering. Eventually, it lost all shock value. The squirrels got used to it.

He noses around the juniper bush, looking for something to roll in to mask his scent. It's unlikely that he'll need to sneak up on an unsuspecting deer today, but it's best to be prepared.

Later, under the uninterrupted riots in her ceiling, the man's hands on Cecily's body anneal by letting her want something she actually has. It moves her forward through frozen jambs. She knows it's not going to work for long, but the hollow wrongness his touch inspires, her vague interest in the textures and responses: these at least prove she is still alive. Too much lately, she hasn't been sure.

After he's gone, she says: all right, Dog?

Dog opens one eye, rolls it. Goes back to sleep.

When they'd come to look at the lake house, the woman who'd lived there for years had showed them around.

"I'm sorry to go," she said. "It's just this new relationship. He has kids, we need more space. Otherwise I'd never leave. Waking to this lake every morning is a treasure."

"I bet," Cecily answered.

The house was a Victorian gingerbread with a bright living room and kitchen, a sun porch. A spiral stair rose to a master bedroom and balcony over the lake; a huge finished basement made a second bedroom and office. The lake began right across the street. A two mile loop trail around it. Many miles of trails in the plains beyond. She knew the village from looping the lake in long years past, but now imagines living in it, really putting down roots again, with Dog. They've moved so much for her teaching gigs, her fellowships and colonies. He's getting too old for the peripatetic life, as she is.

It could be a retirement home for him: he's turning ten now and still beefcake, still athletic—but slowing, stiffening. He's going blind. It's gradual enough that he's mostly unaware of it, but Cecily saw the increase of silver across his eyes and took him to New Hampshire, to their beloved vet Doc, who said it was retinal clouding. They'd talked over the options, more complex and difficult than cataract surgery.

Just think about what you do and why you do it, Doc had said. Blindness in an old dog is not the worst thing. He's so well trained he'll heel to you by voice and hike safely even if he can't see a thing and isn't wearing a leash. Or, you spend thousands of dollars to build him bionic eyes, put him through the surgery, then what? He chases the squirrel he can suddenly see clear as day again, and blows out an elderly knee. Who did you do a favor, there?

About the lake house, Dog was alight with hope. The fenced yard, the trails. The water. He tap-danced on the golden oak floors. He made himself clear.

"You'll be happy here," the woman said, certain. "The State Forest is five minutes that way."

Cecily thought happiness in this place was very possible. Signed the lease the next day, in spite of the creepy landlord and the steep rent, thinking: some things are worth paying for.

Their first morning, waking, staring out the window at the lake right there, Cecily and Dog said in unison:

Holy shit. We live here.

And they went out into it.

Alight.

The man was back to visit and they were hiking the State Forest, on the last ascent to the top, when he asked her if she'd been in love with the one who disappeared a few months back.

Cecily didn't answer, just made the hard left turn into the narrow track to the overlook. Bounded on both sides by dense, almost solid growth of mountain laurel tall enough to create a long and blind alley, the trail opened onto a narrow cliff shelf and an expansive view of the valley floor. She and Dog climbed out onto the sturdy stone, sprawled in the cold air of early spring. The man came and sat beside them.

"Were you in love with him," he asks again, after a time.

She considers being annoyed by the question, considers several snarky responses. Instead, she says: "Well, when you put it that simply, the simple answer is yes, I was. At least, I mostly was. I knew better, so I never let go entirely, but it didn't really help."

Dog had been in love with him, too. And with his big, goofy dog Mutt, who was a bit of an airhead, but a sporty one who was a good snuggler and only very occasionally cranky. Their walks, their meals, their movies watched in tangled piles, the humans' lovemaking: completely uncomplicated forward motion. They'd made a fine pack, they all thought, in spite of their substantive differences. Or most of them did, anyway. When they didn't think it over too carefully and just walked forwards, that is. And when they weren't arguing. And when they weren't crashing into complete mutual incomprehension of unshared priorities, born of wildly different class backgrounds. And when they weren't bickering about respective emotional ages and modes of communication. His waffles, for example. They were the fluffiest in the world, and he radiated joy when he made waffles. Dog and Mutt also radiated joy when they had waffle-balancing competitions on their noses. Cecily had canine-simple joy that dripped with maple syrup, local, dark, and sweet, licked from her face by any one of them, depending on the Sunday.

"Why does it matter," Cecily asked the man on the overlook. "I'm working on getting over it."

He didn't answer, so they sat in companionable silence.

Dog leaned in on Cecily's shoulder: she put her arm around him and scratched his chest, the greying vortex at the heart. He purred.

She was watching cloudshadows skim the opposite side of the valley when Dog stiffened, pulled away, and transformed.

A sound she'd never heard from him or any other living being rumbled out from his body: lower than bass, lower than basso profundo, rising in volume and intensity and vibrating through her bones. He stood on his toes, the bones of his feet arching and claws gripping the granite. Every hair on his body stood on end, and his ruff flipped forward: nothing as mundane as risen hackles, but a viscerally lupine version of a frilled lizard flipped forward. He quadrupled in size, Dog did, and every tooth emerged, lips pulled far back along black-speckled gums, long white canines flashing and curled muzzle spit-flecked. He danced forward on his toes, turned slightly sideways, toward the trailhead, where the head and shoulders of an enormous black bear had just emerged.

The thing about black bears is that they generally avoid conflict in all but two situations: perceived threat to cubs, or this—an enclosed space, from which there is no easy way to back down.

Dog and Cecily had sung the bears of this forest so many times—to let them know they were coming so everyone could avoid each other—that every bear in a twenty mile radius had to know every song Ella Fitzgerald ever recorded. This was just a stupid mistake: she and Dog and the man had been silent and still, the bear had rambled softly out to the overlook as innocently as they had, and now they all were stuck: a narrow, solid-walled path leading to a plunge down a cliff, or confrontation.

The bear curled its lip, hissed.

The man said: "Wha—"

Cecily had only seconds to process how very badly this could go: one swipe from that bear paw and over the cliff Dog would go. She started to rise to put herself in between, but Dog dropped his voice even lower and floated closer to the bear without any apparent motion in his stiff and mysteriously massive legs, and awe overtook her.

This was not the Dog she knew. This was Dog Beast. Wolf Dog. Dog God. Inugami. Anubis the dog-headed god of the dead. Making a sound fit only for underworlds, a skin-raising, soul-freezing sound.

Dog lowered his head, unblinking. You have no chance, Bear, he said.

The bear agreed.

It froze, it silenced, it began to back up. Dog issued another series of sound-waves designed to turn livers to water, and the bear's nose vanished backwards up the trail. They heard it blundering backwards the entire way, crashing its butt into laurel and course-correcting, until it hit the main trail, turned, and ran.

Dog dropped his fur and his lips, his ears and his shoulders, shrank by four sizes, and trotted back to Cecily and the man, cool as a cucumber and twice as relaxed.

He parked himself back at Cecily's shoulder, and looked out over the valley as though nothing at all had happened. When she and the man just sat there like slack-jawed idiots, he pawed her hand to indicate that she really should be scratching his chest again.

Which she did, stunned.

Back at the lake house, they cooked him a steak. Cecily sent the man home after that. She needed to be alone with Dog, to figure out how to acknowledge what she'd just witnessed.

I had no idea, Cecily said. No idea you could say anything like that, Dog. Or change—I am so—god, I am so awed by you.

She threw her arms around him and held him so tightly it was irritating.

Squeezed breathless, Dog suggested they watch some Poirot.

They both liked David Suchet in the part very much indeed.

It was on Martha's Vineyard, staying at his sister's empty house in the off-season, that the man's bipolar mania emerged, wrecking the final day and trip home from what had been a non-stop beach party for Dog: a radiant blur of sticks so salt-heavy they made his lips burn, weird-smelling creatures in interesting shells, clam chowder at least once a day, and fast Labs of all three colors. He fell exhausted and blissed out at the close of each ocean sunset, and Cecily thrilled for him, painfully conscious—watching him so joyous, watching him so unable to see the sticks the other dogs saw or to run as fast as they could when for a decade, he'd left the world in his dust—that there might not be many more ocean trips for Dog.

"Thank you," she said to the man, "for bringing us here. It means the world to me that he got to have three days like this, in this place."

He shrugged, twitchy. Snapped that they were going to miss the ferry, which they didn't, but which they rode separately, rejoining only for the drive home.

By the end of that car ride, it was the end. He was yelling. Twitching. Delusional. Reeking sharp gun-smoke sparks. Paranoid.

He was frightening Dog.

Cecily and Dog walked the lake-loop. Millennia past, a glacier had perched on this part of western Massachusetts: when it melted and traveled the way they do, it created a unique pocket of fauna and flora. A xeric glacial outwash, sandy and acid. Pine and fir, abundant ladyslippers and bloodroot. More than four hundred species of butterflies and moths not found elsewhere in the region. Unlikely snakes, including the hognose, which pretended to be a rattler until that didn't work to scare off a threat, at which point it faked its own death and collapsed, emitting a foul stench: Dog stepped on one once, and was deeply mortified by the resulting histrionics. Lupine of peculiar shape: rather than the usual spikes and cones of dark, rich purple, the lake lupine grew on thin and elegant stalks, in carousels of pink, purple, and yellow. Parti-lupine, Cecily called it. Abundant turtles of every description: snappers, painted, box.

She got a trail bike, re-set Dog's safety training: he took such joy in their four, five, sometimes seven mile rides that she had to install a speedometer to make sure he was going a reasonable speed for an old man. He heeled with flawless perfection, never crossing in front, even when a panicked rabbit broke cover at the last second and zigzagged in front of him for a good fifty yards before it finally dodged off the trail.

How good you are, Cecily breathed. No way I would have been that good.

After their rides, they dropped in the lake to cool and rest, sprawled together in the shallows. Dog's buoyancy was changing, so for real swims, she brought out the PFD she'd gotten for him after a bad injury, when one of his legs would cramp up without warning: it was flowered and had a handle at the top of his spine, so it made him look both incredibly chic and like a Kate Spade handbag. He seemed relieved by its extra support, and became once again the lake hydrofoil, zooming across the surface at great speed.

Though most puppies annoyed him now, he began mentoring the new beagle-border collie-something neighbor, who was a crackpot of precisely the sort Dog had been as a youth, and who thought Dog was the most amazing being in the entire world, whom everyone should strive to be. Cecily agreed, and gave the pup standing welcome at her house.

Dog was written up flatteringly in the village newspaper, alongside Goose, the twenty-three year old Cairn who ran the place, and Falcon, the cancer-lumped blind Lab of enormous grin and equivalent goodwill. They stopped and chatted with Goose and his human a couple of times a week on the way to the Post Office, checking in on how his heart meds were going: "They've taken five years off his age," his human would say. "He's downright perky."

Falcon and his human they saw on almost every night-walk. Falcon would be wandering about bumping into things and smiling, his man would be sitting on the Bridge of Names smoking a joint. "Hey," Cecily would call out so Bob wouldn't get paranoid, "it's just us." And Bob would insist they stop and sit for a few, and he'd tell them the story, again, of how Falcon pushed him out of the way of a bus when Bob was drunk, getting hit himself instead.

"He saved me," Bob would say.

"I know," Cecily would answer. "He loves you."

Or the story of how he was sitting in the cellar with a gun under his chin once, and Falcon came down and looked at him for a long time with such sadness that Bob put the gun down and kept going.

"He saved me," he would say.

"I know," Cecily would answer. "He's a good dog."

Falcon died that winter. Bob went missing.

They never saw him again.

On night-walks, even when the moon was full and spilling silver everywhere to brighten the ground, Cecily had to start bringing a flashlight to shine the way for Dog, who otherwise would stumble in failing vision. Or, she'd keep him on the flat and sandy part, doubling back and forth so they could get some distance without entangling roots, or the complicated rock-bridge over the inlet, or worse, the dangerously slippery tree-bridge they'd built with Mutt and his man, their man, when the pack was one, if only briefly.

Cecily's work took off. On school days, Dog sometimes stayed home, sometimes came to class with her, where he made polite rounds, nodding and smiling, then parked himself in front of her desk for the duration. On home days, grading and editing, Dog would come to her at the computer and say: Cecily. It's time you got outside. And if she didn't come right away, he'd give her ten minutes, then come back and smack her leg. She'd set it all down and go outside, and they'd walk, and walk, or go for shortening bike rides, or go swimming, or go to the State Forest and sing the bears Ella Fitzgerald's Fortieth Birthday Concert Live in Rome from start to finish.

People hit on her, and Cecily ignored it or turned them down.

The daily sweetness of Dog, of work, both requiring more and more attentive love, more intentional building-up and investment, allowing nothing but normalcy and peace in Dog's life and focus on what moved her forward in her own: this is what mattered to her now.

In the fall, she takes him back to New Hampshire for his annual check-up.

Doc says: "He's fit and strong, look at him—and just the right slimness to keep the arthritis from getting too bad." He says: "I am VERY happy about his beautiful teeth. No one has nicer teeth at his age." He says: "A dog of his size, this healthy and well-cared for, should certainly live twelve or fourteen years."

Cecily's brain screeches to a halt.

Dog was past eleven. Twelve was next year.

She rewinds the tape.

Erases it.

Reminds Dog, on their drive home, that when he was a puppy they had discussed this, and he had promised her seventeen years.

Dog's head is out the window, his unfocused eyes reflecting only the silver of a cold and overcast sky, a tapetum of cloud. He isn't trying to see. He's just savoring scent, the onrush of everything.

Your nose, Cecily whispers to him. My ship's prow.

When they get home, the lake has frozen. Just a scrim now, but thickening.

It is an alive thing, ice. It sings. The depths of the lake shift and the surface screams, or cracks with the sound of cannon-fire. Sometimes it moans and cries, or mutters. Always, it speaks: when the temperature drops very fast, its voice is like arrows shot from a quiver, deadly and accurate.

Coming right for you.

BEARS

Cecily was sitting on the pool's edge, goggles in hand, legs in the water.

This happened a long time ago:

She'd gone to the pool counting laps in her head, planning the balance of pull buoy and kick, reaching already for the hungry mile. So when she saw the bear hogging the available lane, floating on its back like some kind of lazy Esther Williams, she'd simply been annoyed. How to get the bear to move without losing much time from the lap-swimming hour?

When the bear rolled onto its side and ogled her with intent, though, she'd realized this was a situation that required some real presence of mind. She gazed back at the bear; sidelong enough not to be rude, but rudely enough to set the boundary. She was here to swim, not to mess around.

The bear did not take her point. Instead, it began to swim toward her, leaving a perfect wedge of nose-wake, then stopped just inches away, treading water, and stared at her, eyes glittering with humor and invitation. She stared back.

What, she'd said.

The bear sent a jet of water from its mouth splashing across her lap.

I'm here to swim, Cecily had said, stern. It's serious.

The bear huffed, snorted, smacked the goggles hard out of her hand; they shot across the surface of the water, then sank.

Hey! Cecily had shouted.

This is happening now:

The bear rises up out of the water with a powerful kick, raises a massive paw, and strikes Cecily hard at her hairline, claws ripping through her skin, down the center of her face and chest, through her abdomen and pubis. There is very little blood, somehow, and when the bear strips her skin off like a banana peel, what is left in her is laughter.

All exposed muscle now, leaking plasma, she rises to dive, submerge, entangle with wet fur and musk.

I thought bears hated chlorine, she says, giggling, then the bear dunks her, grips her hard and pulls her under where she does not need to breathe.

Cecily goes to the dog pound, one hundred eighty five cages in a long, low, concrete bunker. She is riven. Can't eat, can't sleep: her familiar run down in the road, on purpose, three months back. She has shrunk to bone and ash. This is her last chance.

It should never have happened: dead end dirt road, fifteen mile an hour speed limit—

"He's done it before," her neighbor had said, too late. "He kills dogs for sport."

"You tell me this now," Cecily had whispered, dying.

Familiar bones feed the Japanese maple her fiancé had given her for an engagement present. It had been in a pot until they moved, carrying boxes, his body, a shovel to dig his early grave. Now it grew wildly, visibly; rapid, vibrant inches fed by his flesh.

She would cancel the wedding soon, and her mother would say: "He was your child, really, and lots of couples don't survive the death of their child—"

Cecily would answer: "He wasn't our child, he was more and other than that, he was my familiar, I saved him, and he saved me—"

Her mother would say: "I know, I'm just saying—"

And Cecily would say: "I know Mom, but please, don't, I just—I can't stand it."

She slept in the next room, when she slept: she shrank and shrank, and the smaller she got the more her fiancé wanted to fuck her emerging bones. How he praised her for shrinking. For dying.

This man, Cecily understood after nearly a decade of these kinds of unkindnesses together, is my enemy.

She shrank and shrank, she could not stop. It had her by the throat.

So many things, for a long time, they'd done well together. Core things. Primal things. The making of home, one other people wanted to come to. Travelling. Great sex. They made good containers, the two of them, to put other things into, but they did not really like each other, and the cruelty was a polluting thread. By the end, Cecily cut him as often as he cut her, blades between them always, even when her emerging bones slid, slick with death and desperate hope for some salvageable remains, in his grip.

This is stupid, she began to know. Plain stupid and mean. This is not who or how you want to be. Her familiar, murdered. Her fiancé, lusting her death. Her, starving herself to bone. The sound of knives sharpening in every silence.

They went to the pound.

Lots of people in failing relationships get an animal, Cecily knew. Or they make a baby.

They'd been talking about both. Desperately seeking cement. Distraction. Adhesive of shared responsibility.

Cecily chose the high-risk pound rather than the posh no kill shelters, or reproduction.

"Let's go where they need us most," she'd said. "Where maybe we can do some real good."

In the concrete bunker, dogfight survivors, trained from the beginning to kill other dogs. One after another, loving the human hand but lunging for the throat of her friend's gentle mastiff, brought along to test this very thing.

After heartbroken hours, she sent her friend's dog with her fiancé back to the car, said goodbye to the beautiful, scarred Rottweilers, Pit Bulls, Dobermans, mutts of large stature and thick musculature. Weeping for them, wretched that she knew she could not save them, that they could not save her. Everywhere in her life, dogs. Nowhere in her life, the resources to help these badly wounded creatures who could not stop hurting each other.

She headed for the door, still weeping.

"YOU," someone shouted at her back. "STOP."

Cecily stopped, turned.

"Come here," the woman behind the counter in the lobby said.

Cecily did.

The woman ducked out of sight, rose with something in her arms.

"Take this one," she said.

Between her hands, a black lump resembling, if anything recognizable, a Kalamata olive pit someone had chewed thoroughly then spat out, lumpy and pointy. Scowling.

The pound woman's hands under his front paws exaggerated his fat puppy belly. His wrinkled brow, as yet un-grown-into, exaggerated the Mussolini expression. Everything about his face disgruntled, outraged.

I am cold, Dog said to Cecily. I am alone. My pack is missing, and I am too furious to be afraid. Who the fuck are you and what are you looking at, anyway?

Cecily wiped tears and snot from her face.

Laughed out loud.

Hello, she said. You're awfully small to be out on your own.

"He's seven weeks old," the pound woman said. "Mother is a Dalmatian. Another casualty of that goddam movie. Father unknown. She was abandoned hugely pregnant, left tied to a lamppost in Chicopee. I took her home so the puppies could be born somewhere without kennel cough. They're on solid food now, and I don't have room. There are ten. They have to go. He's the first one out."

The size of a loaf of bread.

The soul of an epic.

Cecily took Dog into her arms.

"Sometimes you have to start at the beginning," the pound woman says.

All struggle and tension, this puppy. All elbows and knees. Bony, the two of them, with soft parts here and there in spite of themselves.

Disgruntlepup, she croons. Shhh.

You're not my Mom, Dog says.

No, Cecily laughs. I'm not.

It begins.

Neither of them have any idea what has just happened. How much.

A couple of weeks later, once he's vaccinated and well-started on training—which proves extremely difficult not because he's not smart, but because he's a smartass—she takes him on his first outing.

The Charlemont Pow Wow isn't very big, but it's sweet: concessions, silversmiths, a couple of painters, dance competitions. People smile at Dog, heeling ostentatiously on his new purple leash, tiny and vast, a Very Important Being. He has decided heeling makes good sense, though he won't admit publicly that he finds the proximity of Cecily's legs protective.

After a couple of hours, he collapses from overstimulation and fry-bread crumbs, falls face-first into the grass and snores. Cecily picks him up and carries him sleeping in the crook of her arm, his nose pressed wetly into her neck. She can only hold him this way when he's asleep: the rest of the time he won't tolerate it. Too patronizing.

Pail Face John waves from the Veteran's booth, where he is selling his memoir. Cecily wanders over, chats for a while about all things jewelry, recovery and keeping healthy, writing, sales.

"Nice dog," the man who'd been sitting near them says when John gets up to talk to another acquaintance.

"Yes," Cecily answers. "He's a good one." She looks down at the bundle of iridescent black in her arms, each shaft of hair as blue and purple as it is black, true raven fur. She is suddenly aware of his heartbeat on hers, how the two have synchronized; his infant-beats are triple her speed, but synchronized. She is suddenly aware of his breath moving in and out of his body in hot, gentle bursts that hit her skin and penetrate, moving into and through her bloodstream. She is suddenly aware of his mortality. She is suddenly terrified, and death-struck. Cecily stares at Dog's paw: still snoring, he has stretched his webbed feet and the light pours through translucent skin, plum-colored and fragile.

The man peers at her face closely, peers at Dog, stands. He is tall. Scarecrow-skinny. He wears a red baseball cap from the VFW. He fishes something out of his pocket.

"Take this," he says, and inserts a red-wrapped tobacco charm into the palm of her left hand under Dog's sleeping body. "It's a blessing, that's all. To keep him safe. Pin it where he sleeps."

Cecily opens her mouth to say thank you, but her throat closes and tears spill.

"This one'll live a long, happy life," the man says, tenderly.

Cecily, who is not superstitious, but who is skinless, clears her throat. Clears it again. Says, urgent and blood-fierce, if quietly: "Exactly how long?"

The man frowns.

"He'll live a long life," he repeats.

Not long enough, Cecily knows, her heart racing breakneck.

She pins the red cloth bag of tobacco to his bed that night. For the next twelve years, everywhere he sleeps, she pins it.

Mostly, that means her own bed. Sometimes, his travel bed.

She is not superstitious, but she is skinless. It's a blessing, that's all. She pins it.

Not long enough.

"Temporal scramble of the olfactory variety," Cecily will say to her visiting friend on the trail down to the water, to explain her sudden stop, her stillness mid-stride. "Sorry. It was the aspens. The hot dust."

"It's okay," her friend, who knows, will say. "We can wait."

Dog, under Mount Greylock, his rear feet knuckling when he walked, nerve impulses scrambled, pain tearing through him. August. His final weeks. How he stood as if braced against some ferocious internal wind buffeting him.

By the river, these many thousands of miles and two years forward from his death, there will be a black dog retrieving sticks in the glacial flow, his powerful kicks crossing fierce currents of joy. Cecily will feel nothing when she looks at him.

"Nice dog," she'll say.

It will have become normal, the screaming absence. The fact that nothing comes close.

What is it that you need from me, Cecily shouts at the ceiling, when Dog's frantic, spring-coiled hubris breaks her patience.

He is a madhouse on four feet.

He's growing as fast as the Japanese maple in the yard, apparent inches a day.

He vibrates: electric with attention always.

He chases the mastiff endlessly, biting up and down the enormous dog's ankles. They take to calling him The Perforator. The peaceable giant ignores it until blood starts to flow, then eventually slaps Dog to the floor with a massive paw, lies down on him and pins him under an arm, holding him there until the puppy calms.

He gets into boxing matches with the cat, who is not entirely sure this is funny, but who is determined, perhaps unhealthily, to win.

He sprints in circles around the house, and will not listen.

Cecily can see that a lot of this is just unspent energy. He is also an apparent genius with a problematic gift for picking up English words and phrases after hearing them a couple of times—and, she recognizes, he is a completely unscarred, normal, demanding, bossy little shithead who requires something from her she has not yet figured out before he will see why he should take her word for anything.

Large affection between them already, but tension and struggle, too.

Something in each of them held in reserve.

Fine, Cecily says. Tomorrow morning, we go out walking, and we do not stop until YOU decide to stop. We're going to see what it takes to tire you sane, you little Cretin.

It takes ten miles, by her pedometer.

Fuck, says Cecily, when Dog finally flops over, panting happily. This is bad.

Dog grins, flops on his back, boxes the air.

Cecily laughs.

She starts walking him five miles a day, holding a long stick above shoulder-height. Dog does jumping jacks the whole way, trying to catch it. She figures this doubles his distance.

She puts him in boot camp, and ratchets up his training. He eats from her hand; every meal her scent. She teaches him to go through doors behind her, never in front, and that if he wants up or down off something, he is to ask: there will be no crackpot hurtling-without-looking that lands him in front of a truck, or sends him off a cliff. No caprice between them, but no disrespect, either. She obsesses about his safety, imagining every horror she can think of and training him away from those things: everything she imagines, she prevents. The horrors that will happen, she did not even imagine.

Heel and sit and down he had by eight weeks. She adds 'slap me four' for a high-comedy handshake, passing in the halls; 'slap me eight' for both paws high. She teaches him to ring a bell on the door when he wants to go out. To speak, then to bark once for 'no,' twice for 'yes.' To stay for long stretches while she walks hundreds of feet away with his stick, then to fire his engines and fly when she raises it, pulling it from the air at the moment she releases. To balance a book on his head, a slice of cheese on his nose. To stay in heel with rapid and unpredictable changes in speed and direction, both on and off leash: while running up and down stairs, going around trees, while rabbits scatter nearby and are ignored, stopping on a dime, racing ahead with no warning. He keys in deeply to her body language, and she to his: every cue is speed-read, used.

More and more, they become one being in two bodies. He bores easily, smart and wired: she occupies his mind constantly, creating puzzles for him to solve out of every activity.

She teaches him 'turn around,' which, given his spring-coil nature, quickly becomes a form of dance; so she teaches him to salsa, and merengue.

How his raven-black shines when he dances.

The diamond glint of infinite life. Of joy.

This happened a long time ago:

Cecily had been walking a forest trail alone, loamy earthy springing beneath her feet, when she tripped over an exposed root and went down. Instinctively, she'd put her hands out in front of her to break the fall, but when they touched the ground, it wasn't there and she plummeted into a deep cave underground, landing in a painful crash on wet and cluttered stone.

The cave was dark and granite, walls and root-hung ceiling dripping water. The floor was littered with bones. On the farthest bare wall, a painted jaguar.

This is happening now:

The jaguar wakes, growls, turns in a blur of bunched muscle and black iridescence, and leaps from the wall into Cecily's body, knocking her down and tearing her chest open. It paces around her, tail lashing, while she bleeds and waits to die. It strikes her again, this time without claws. Again. Quick punches, punctuated by stamping and low rumbles in the back of its dark throat.

Get up off the ground, you useless coward, it says. Stop the cave's tears.

Cecily pushes herself to her knees. The wound is both deep, to her heart, and symbolic: she is not dying, it just hurts like it. She rises, wobbling, to her feet.

But how—

The jaguar hisses.

Cecily pulls down root-ends in wrist-thick and hair-fine strands and weaves a clumsy bucket to catch the dripping water. She doesn't know what to do with it: the water is everywhere, the tears won't stop. They are too many. The jaguar paces and threatens, impatient and dangerous. Cecily puts the bucket in the center of the cave floor, where one drip among thousands lands in its porous gesture, its symbolic catch.

The falling water slows, stops.

The jaguar bares teeth and leaps again, knocking Cecily flat against granite.

Assemble the bones, it says.

Oh god, Cecily, I don't—

Claws flay her back. Blood pours.

Cecily begins gathering the bones. For days, years, millennia, there she crawls, from slimy bone to slimy bone, trying one out against another, a calcium jigsaw puzzle moldered and gristly, reeking in her hands: when she finds the right fit for each tiny part, it sticks to the rest. The jaguar circles and threatens when she pauses. Finally, her skeleton is assembled. With unexpected tenderness for this sorry assemblage she has made, Cecily props it against the wall, crossing the legs and adjusting the head so it can have a clear view of the cave. Then she lies down, exhausted.

The jaguar's not having it.

It screams murder, and sinks teeth into the back of Cecily's neck, lifting and shaking her, then hurling her into the blank granite wall where she crumples, falls to the ground.

Tell the story, it demands. Say what happened.

No, Cecily says. I can't.

The jaguar goes still. Drops low to the ground. Its tail quivers once, muscles vibrating.

You will, it says. Or you will die.

Kill me then. Cecily says. I CAN'T. And even if I can, I don't want to.

PAINT, the jaguar says, every fine shaft of fur sparking black and blue and purple.

No.

NOW.

Cecily pulls herself up into a sitting position, her bleeding back against the cool granite.

Fuck you, she says.

Claws rake across her face, opening her to bone. The pain is blinding. In her blood-covered hands, charcoal. She is too tired to fight.

She turns to the wall.

I can't draw for shit, you know, she mutters, and begins: a crude sketch of the wolf who raised her, who ran himself ragged trying to keep her safe, who like all beings who love other mortal beings, failed to do so.

I hate this, she says, and the jaguar hisses again. Yeah, yeah, I know, Cecily says. Fuck you. I'm doing it. She draws and draws, filling inches, feet, whole rock-faces.

The cats, legion, abandoned by students in the college town and fed by Cecily as a child until they came in floods, feral and ravenous, lavish with love for this thin child with dark circles under her eyes. Her mother, unconscious at her father's hands, or at her own, gallons of Almaden in the sideboard cupboard where Cecily could steal it to make herself sleep, to silence the nightmares and knock herself out, too. Dying, all of them. Walls of books: the beautiful, terrible, other-worlds within. Cecily putting her own flesh between the monster and everyone else, to protect them: how this somehow worked, though it worked at great cost. Her father, brilliant and probably fatal, in fields of wildflowers, forests growing up through abandoned houses discovered with wonder between glittering episodes of coke and vodka fueled horror. The scars inside her own body, laid layer upon layer across her child-heart, cervix, mind. The safety of stone walls, laid rock by rock with her grandfather, his large hands over hers, placing them to last. The stillness of forest, the height of trees: the sound the leaves at the very top made when Cecily climbed as high as the bending trunk would allow and sat perfectly still, for hours, deer and bobwhites and bears passing below, peregrines above. The thousand deaths. The thousand gifts that keep a child alive: kittens, fierce prides of murderous glee. The teachers who let her run ahead, her painful boredom a glorious opportunity to those few good teachers with something real to offer. The pool, to which she walked at seven in the morning, and from which she did not return until eight at night, every summer, even at five, six years old—the smell of chlorine the certainty of well-being and simplicity, the possibility of simply having pleasure in the moment. The burn of hallucinations, always horrific but preferable to reality nonetheless: the burn of what it cost to get those hallucinogenics. The certainty of death by fifteen, her own skin too painful a place to live. Her first voluntary lover, whose intuitive gentleness restored her sexuality to her own sovereignty instead of laying down more scars. The solace of animal bodies, soft and vulnerable as hers, lithe muscle and sharp teeth like hers, wary of humans and wisely so, feral like her, complete in their loyalty and congruence. The inexplicable moment of wanting to live, and the transformation that took place in that moment. The gate she walked through then. The one that led to a forest path where she tripped and fell into a cave.

That's enough, Cecily says, and drops the charcoal. If it's not enough for you, I can't help that. I told the truth. The sketches flicker and move. Everything happens. The wolf comes closer to Cecily. The cats, too. Peregrines. Bears. They gather at the center. Cecily stares at the wall, her back to the cave.

The jaguar rumbles low in its throat.

Stop it, please, Cecily whispers. I can't do any more.

You don't have to, the jaguar answers, and then Cecily is surrounded by the jaguar's body: it has hurled itself at her, rolling her into a perfect ball inside its grip, and is curled now on the floor, Cecily wrapped in its vast paws, against the curve of its belly, her face pushed into its neck.

It smells of flowers, the way kittens do—but a precise floral musk Cecily has never encountered: gardenias are the closest thing, but it's food, this smell, and life itself with enough truth to contain death. Perfect, silent joy indistinguishable from peace. She breathes it in. It permeates her memory.

For years, for decades, for her life, she will remember this smell, and seek it.

The glitter of black, iridescent fur.

The slow heartbeat of a god at rest, and pleased.

Wrapped in jaguar—one being now in two bodies, their single heartbeat the drum of the world—Cecily sleeps.

It is the safest she has ever been.

When Dog becomes hysterical, which is less and less often as he grows and settles, but still a regular occurrence, Cecily scoops him up and stuffs his nose into her neck, or armpit, or the crook of her elbow, where her blood is close to the surface. He writhes and squirms for a moment, then huffs in her scent deeply, deeper, more slowly, and calms.

One day she realizes this chemical trick might work on her, too: she's trying to read the thousands of pages her graduate work is requiring of her when he decides he's bored and starts diving on and off the daybed where she's sprawled with papers and stacks of books. On and off, on and off, isn't it hilarious, skidding and bouncing, and her stuff flies everywhere—she grits her teeth, picks him up and stuffs his face into her neck, then stuffs her own face into his armpit and breathes in deeply.

Jesus, Cecily says, stunned. Your smell. I didn't—

Dog writhes, irritated. She flips him onto his back on the daybed and buries her face in his belly, breathing. He laughs.

How did I not know this about you until now, Cecily breathing his skin, breathing home.

Dog, wriggling, bites her shirt-sleeve and wrestles it. Not know what, he mumbles, mouth full of cotton.

He smells of gardenias. Under the fur, under the accretions of cold grass and goldenrod, dust bunnies from surfing under the couch, his skin: he smells of flowers.

You smell like an angel Gabriel García Márquez made up, she says, flooding with love.

They are entirely safe.

I'm still bored, he says, and bites her braid, giggling and yanking.

One day, while boxing, he bites the cat: instinctively, Cecily bites the bridge of his nose, hard. He drops to his belly immediately, submits to the cat and Cecily both.

The cat slaps Dog, and stomps away.

Oh, Cecily says. I see how it is. You want real wolfing.

Dog rolls onto his back and wags his tail.

Okay, Cecily says. I can do that.

She takes him on a long, snowy hike, after which he falls asleep in his Christmas bed near the woodstove, lined with purple velvet since he is such a monstrous little king.

Cecily is drinking eggnog sprinkled with nutmeg.

She considers Dog, who is on his back, hind legs splayed and one paw straight up in the air: this is his favorite sleeping position. She tiptoes up to him, takes a big mouthful, lowers her face to his, and dribbles the eggnog onto his lips.

He wakes, opens his eyes wide, stunned.

She dribbles more, and some more: he laps the eggnog as it drips from her wolf mouth. His eyes go vague and out of focus, overwhelmed.

Communion.

Cecily feels all the tumblers line up, the locks open.

There is nothing between them now.

She takes him to parades and introduces him to bagpipes, drums corps, trumpets. She takes him up escalators and down elevators. She gets permission from bus drivers to have him sit in the stairwell while puffs of air brakes hiss and doors open and close. They go in and out and in and out and around and around revolving doors, laughing like maniacs. Every weird or potentially frightening thing she can think of she teaches him how to do with joy. Fireworks mean fried dough and glow-necklaces. Sirens mean sit and wait. Gunshots mean heel immediately, but without worry. Thunder means a spur of the moment rain-walk, or an explosion of hide-and-seek kibble. Crosswalks mean sit until Cecily says *okay go!* She teaches him 'stalk' so he can creep soundlessly through the woods with her, hardly crackling a leaf as they steal up close to spy on deer. She teaches him he may never chase another creature without permission: occasionally, when it's safe for everyone, she gives him permission. She teaches him to bark at the squirrels who live in the ceiling upon the shouted command "CRIMINAL!" and for several years, this remains one of the funniest things in the world.

Hyper-vigilant, stern, she introduces him to a porcupine they find sitting on a low branch, just above Dog's head.

This, Cecily says to Dog, is a very pointy animal. This is a very dangerous animal. This, she says, is a very gentle animal. Look at its beautiful hands. You will never, ever chase one of these.

Dog cocks his head, sniffs the nearby animal while maintaining a polite avoidance of eye contact. The porcupine's chocolate nose sniffs back.

All right, Cecily, Dog says. I believe you.

He is never quilled.

Cecily leaves her fiancé two weeks before the wedding.

In the end, the end is very kind. He is relieved, which relieves her, and they part quite gently, wishing each other well. Sort out the house and the stuff and the entanglements of long years gradually. Everything amicable and fair.

"There's one thing," she says.

"What's that," he asks.

"Dog," she says. "He's mine. We are not negotiating this."

There is no argument.

Everyone knows how it is.

When it's just Dog and Cecily in the house they build new rituals, just for the Us of them.

Every night before sleep, they open the bedroom window wide, and lean as far out of it as they can together. Cecily hoots softly, and the Great Horned Owl who lives in the tree nearby hoots back. Dog wags fervently, his whole body keyed forward, listening. She hoots again. The owl answers.

Owl, baby, listen, Cecily breathes, and Dog vibrates with magic.

They keep these conversations going for twenty minutes, some nights.

He usually falls asleep before she does.

She watches him, drifting. He looks more bear than wolf, in sleep. She loves this about him.

It can't have ended this way, Cecily will think, his still form on the vet's floor in her arms, ruff soaked with an epic's flood, cleaned of everything his body let go when his heart stopped, the palm of her left hand burning with the world-ending softness of his last breath, which she caught and held, which she pressed into her own chest. It can't have ended. Against his will. His epic, infinite will. To joy. To life. To her.

Both of them.

Extinguished.

She will resist euphemisms.

"This wasn't a 'good death,'" she will say of the word euthanasia.

"He is not 'sleeping,'" she will say.

"He is dead," Cecily will say, "and I killed him."

Us, she will know. I killed Us.

Two years after she kills him, Dog is still there in the next room. She looks over her shoulder, and his ready face is there, open: he lights when her gaze meets his, and smiles with his ears crinkled forward. Her heart bursts with longing.

This is happening now:

Mom, she says, because this isn't real and so her mother can be there: why is he still alive?

We were just talking about that, Cecily's mother says, gesturing at Cecily's army of gathered dead in loose clusters at the edges of the room, crowding. We think it's because he doesn't know he's gone. He only knows he loves you, and you love him.

Some things are stronger than death.

There's a cost, though, to breaking those barriers.

When the last of the house stuff is sorted and it's time, Cecily and Dog drive north looking for a new home. In the Green Mountain National Forest, she finds an abandoned 1830's farmhouse, tracks down the owner, red-eyed and suspicious.

"I want to live in that house you own off Wagon Wheel Road," she says.

"It's trashed," he answers.

"I can see that. But I'll renovate it into rentable condition if you let me live there cheap for a year," she says to his beery, bleary face.

Eventually, they make a deal.

Cecily and Dog pack a truck, move to the top of the mountain deep inside the woods where she grew up.

She bleaches the entire house, including mildewed walls and ceilings. She spackles holes, foam-insulates. She plastics the broken panes until she can replace the glass and re-glaze: loose, the drippy glass vibrates when a cow moose sings. She primes: Dog, helping, gets spots of primer on his ears and back and Cecily shouts: Dalmatian! She mends the chimney-bricks, fallen out of place. She repaints the floorboards upstairs: periwinkle blue where they had been robin's egg. She paints her biggest bookcase to match, makes the walls and ceiling glow bright white. Light spills into the room at night, almost blinding when it's clear. There is one streetlight on the whole mountain, nothing to pollute the sky. Constellations stand in sharp relief, sky-sentinels and story.

They moonlight stroll with coyotes and bears, following the night-tracks of moose. Whitetails trumpet and thunder across star-drenched fields of Queen Anne's Lace. A fisher cat humps along, musky and accordioned.

Autumn turns hoarfrost, hoarfrost turns ice, ice turns snow, blizzard upon blizzard. It drops to forty below and the thermometer explodes, sending mercury splashing across the ice crust, six feet of snow beneath it, silver pooling in a declivity: Cecily bundles, bundles Dog, and they run outside, where Dog pees in a hurry and Cecily scoops thermometer viscera into a can and puts the can in the shed. Back inside, they laugh and laugh, hopping up and down to get warm, eyelashes frozen together.

They spend a year in this forest. Everything happens. They are in their prime. They are terribly vulnerable. There are very few humans involved in the life they make, and there is little work: they are dangerously broke, but completely happy. For a year, they walk, day and night, the forest theirs alone.

When they come down, they are more than ever an interlocking puzzle-box of one being in two bodies.

They have survived what must surely be the worst. They have discovered a series of falling water terraces beaver-built, populated by hundreds of thousands of oak toads. An abandoned apple orchard, still fertile and yielding. Stone cellar holes, mountain lakes. Bobwhites by the thousands, which Cecily gave Dog permission to tree. They have tracked wolves, and stalked a moose for miles, skirting steaming scat the size of tennis balls and watching vast hoof-prints in marshy earth fill with water. The coyotes and trumpeting whitetails are their soundtrack. They have found an ice-shattered tree forming a perfect temple gate they call the Coyote Tori: they have walked through it into the Milky Way itself, spread over them personally, their own private world's quilt.

They are only a hair past halfway, Dog and Cecily.

There is much more to come, he will live a long and happy life. He will work carpentry gigs, teach college at several universities. He will direct community theatre, sitting in his own director's chair and groaning loudly when the actors drop their lines. He will attend parties and get his own plate of blueberry pie. He will make hundreds of friends, become a role model for other dogs. He will be on television, marching in a pride parade and outshining all the queens in his badass leather cap. He will raise money for the pound that gave him. He and Cecily will wake spine to spine every morning, their vertebrae interlocked, breath and pulses synchronized: he will stretch his toes and thump his tail and she will mumble: hello, beloved, roll over to spoon him, and fall back to sleep. He will protect her sleep with vigilance, and guard her from migraines, suggesting she get off the computer and go outside when her screen-time's grown too long, poking her gently in the thigh when her electrical field starts to crackle so she can take a vasoconstrictor. She never taught him to do this, he just figured it out. When grief thickens the air around her and begins to turn to depression-sludge, he coils engagingly, sings, tells jokes, rests his head on her leg and stretches out beside her. She devotes herself to his wellbeing, making every life choice with his joy in mind. No one comes between them, few are fool enough to try. A few become a part of them for a while, then move along: they miss them, usually, but the world is never more complete than when it is just the Us.

They can see it coming, the silvering of retinas, the stiffening, the gradual loss of sight. They make adjustments.

They spend hours in the lake where they settle after Vermont: Dog swims into Cecily's arms and she envelops his vibrating body, joy quivering his flanks. She holds him in the water, and sings to him softly: sometimes he sneaks his nose into her neck and relaxes into the song, sometimes he shoves off her belly with a joyous kick, splashing for another swim around her before launching back into her arms, giggling the way he did as a pup. He becomes honorary president of the Lake Association.

In the State Forest, they find otter skids: at the entrance to one of them, scat composed entirely of fish scales. Dog sees it, starts to shoulder-dive into it, self-corrects and says to Cecily: LOOK! IT'S BEAUTIFUL!

Do it, Dog, she answers. Go ahead. Roll.

He hesitates in disbelief for a moment, then hurls himself into the scales, writhing in ecstasy.

Comes up covered with glitter, head to toe.

He's so beautiful he steals her breath.

Sparkling.

The imminent failure of Dog's central nervous system, the waves of pain shuddering under his skin: this they cannot see coming, and that is a gift.

Those are weeks that will come suddenly, with only one small seizure as harbinger: those are weeks that will sear past in a violence they will neither of them survive.

For a long life, they are the Us.

Not long enough, they both know.

Every day, they know what they have.

Cecily dreams.

This happened a long time ago:

Dog, seventy-seven pounds of shining fur and muscle, a beefcake beauty he showed no indications of becoming as a wee kalamata, uttered a series of echoing barks, vibrating from flews to feathers.

Bear, he said. In the woods. Right there. A bad bear.

There are no bad bears, Dog, Cecily answered.

Dog does not agree. This one is, he growled.

Just leave it be, love, Cecily said, her hand on his back, but Dog lunged, dove from the deck and streaked into the darkness of the woods.

Dog, Cecily cried, suddenly sick with terror, but he was gone: she leapt the deck railing and ran after him, following the chaos-noise of shattering branches, hurricanes of leaves, panting breath and growls.

She couldn't keep up: the fight changed direction every second. Her bipedal frame was slow and clumsy, the few rods and cones she had pulled too little information from the night, her useless nose could not keep up with the battle unfolding in black trees, sentinel and obstructive. Animal bodies gone archetype without her. She couldn't keep up.

She called and called, and when the chaos-noise suddenly ended and complete quiet fell, she froze with bone-dread. In silence, she backed up toward the house, bumping trees that scratched and bit, the blackness hovering, choking.

This is happening now.

Dog, she whispers. Dog. Come back to me, Dog.

He emerges from the forest, walking on three legs, one wounded paw held close to his chest and dragging a vast bear-skin.

It is empty of flesh, a deflated sack of fur.

A whole bear shape with no bear in it anymore.

You're safe now, Cecily, Dog says.

I brought this for you.

You must keep it where you sleep.

It is a blessing.

The Dog Husband

THE BLOSSOM-CARVED BOX was glued shut. She'd tried to open it in the car, in a pull-out on the mountain crest. Pushing and pulling at the slide-top that wouldn't slide, even though she knew if it opened the wind would take the ashes. Unable to stop. Nails tearing. Seeing, finally, through salt, the line of leaked adhesive: rubber cement, maybe. Super glue. Then, the passage of an hour, perhaps minutes, perhaps three hours in buzzing black, and eventual clearing. Putting the box back in the passenger seat, riding shotgun; the window open slightly, to let in the smell of crisping leaves, the gold light. For him.

I cannot imagine, she said, months later, the box digging into her stomach, how anyone will ever know me again.

The box did not speak.

Months later, in woods she'd never visited and so woods she could bear, a man told her stories of the medicine woman who lived in Indian Hollow for decades, her bones hidden after death because people kept trying to steal parts, for healing. His dog told her stories of the excellent comedy of sticks, the urgency of water. The river told stories of how it had once lifted the medicine woman's house and moved it one hundred feet: the neighbors had come and carried it back.

"This is all bloodroot," Cecily said to the man, of both sides of the trail dotted white with scores of splay-fingered petals and silver, curling leaves. "I bet she used this for dyes. I would, anyway."

"It's beautiful," the man said.

"Hard to find," Cecily answered. "Endangered. Poison, though, and it stains everything. You need to be careful. If you even score the surface, it bleeds red for hours."

They visited the stone footprint of the medicine woman's cabin, fieldstone foundation full of pennies. She always said no one owed her anything, but a handful of pennies might be alright, so people gave her pennies for plants, for help. People leave pennies for her still, probably, Cecily thought. I would, anyway, if there was anything I wanted. Bloodroot, or a stick. A drink of the river. The man's dog dove into the collected rainwater in the cellar hole. Dropped flat, wallowed in copper-joy. Radiant.

Later, a bald eagle flew by, close and low. Harassed by a crow, who was winning.

Fist bump in the forest: the man was elated. Rarities everywhere, some days.

"Spirit," he said, of the eagle.

"Or tricks," Cecily said of the corvid.

A nesting peregrine called to her mate, flying wide over the river looking for supper.

"The church-voices of raptors," Cecily noted. "If I could be any of them, I'd be a peregrine. No one else can fly that fast. They could catch a ghost if they wanted."

There was a woman in the far north, much, much farther north than here, who kept turning down the man who wanted her. She and her dog were enough: they slept back to back every night, their spines nesting vertebra by vertebra, an interlocking puzzle. They breathed, dreamed as one being. Stretched and snapped gently back into two bodies each morning, but still, every lock yielded to their shared key. Behind every door, more beauty.

Jealous, the rejected man accused her of loving the dog like a man. He's your dog husband, he spat.

She did not even dignify this vulgarity with a response. There were doors to open. There was beauty.

One day, the man found the dog on his own, and perforated the animal's bones with a million tiny holes.

Your human wife, he told the suffering dog. She's on the other side of the river, and she's in trouble. She needs you to find her.

The dog began to swim, at the bend where the water was deep but the crossing short.

His webbed feet were not enough for his lost buoyancy. He strove for shore, but water filled his skeleton. He didn't make it. It was like his bones had turned to lead.

The woman never recovered.

She may have turned into a bear and mauled all the humans to death, or a deer who charged the hunter's gun, or a water monster who never left that terrible bend of the river and drowned anyone who crossed there. Or maybe she just died. There was something about not being human after that, anyway. Cecily couldn't quite summon up how it ended.

She hated that story.

Cecily splays the pads of her fingers into the spaces between the carved blossoms of the box while she reads. She sleeps with the box at her back. In the mornings, the box does not stretch with her waking, tail thumping and toes extended into the day's possibility: her nervous system lurches along, solitary but for wood pressed into her spine. She does not mind the bruising corners.

Dreaming landscapes of ash, Cecily cuts off great fistfuls of hair, dons the skin of a human, travels thousands of miles into the west, forests and mountains she has not seen before. She teaches epics.

Calls it her "Iliad in the Wilderness" period. Darkness veils her eyes.

Someone she barely knows writes to her: "The truth is, they are all Enkidu," and she can't stop crying.

She is Inanna, a corpse hung from a hook in a stone wall deep underground.

"How do we go on," she asks her classes, "heart-open, in the presence of such terrible vulnerability and loss? In the presence of death? That is the question this story asks of us."

A student writes, glib and bright: "Everyone knows what it is to love deeply, and to lose that love."

"Do they?" Cecily writes back in the margin notes. "Do they *really*?"

Her pen tears a hole in the paper.

Western mountains are loud. Young. Tall and boisterously jagged. Nothing like the elders of the east. The trees, ferns, mosses of the northwest are all just slightly different, unfamiliar even when she knows the species. Some of the black bears are blond, with grizzly claws. Kermodes. The spirit bear. The real grizzlies just north, or occasionally at the local dump. Western coyotes are shrill, Mariah Carey to the east's Tom Waits. The wolves, though, are Nina Simone. And the cougars silent.

Cecily walks and walks in sodden forest, by herself.

"Do you worry about hiking with cougars," she'd asked a Scot who worked at the library and was clearly an outdoorswoman.

"You can't," the woman said. "Here, not going out because of cougars or bears is like not going out because it's raining. Just go. Use common sense, don't hike with earbuds in, but go out. Life is short."

"That's what I figured," Cecily had answered.

Up, and up. Down again. Up again. Orienting to the mountain with the sentinel trees along its ridge, the range over the sound, the caldera-shaped peak, the tusk-shaped peak, the constantly shifting light, the largest piece of freestanding granite aside from Gibraltar, the elaborate peak of the most elaborate mountain—a massive, extinct volcano—for which the vast wilderness is named.

She does not listen for animals. She doesn't try for them, either, but she doesn't listen. If she walks into a bear, or a cougar's teeth pierce the back of her neck and sever her spinal cord, she thinks that would make sense. There isn't much time outside, anyway; all she does now is work. She sees the animals' sign, and sometimes feels them see her, but there are no encounters. She waits, walks, works. There is no one to protect.

Back east, there is nowhere she can go that doesn't cut her. Vermont. Massachusetts. New Hampshire. Maine. New York. There is sign everywhere: spoor of joy, dried into clumps of rabbit fur and bone on trail-boulders, marking what used to be the way, the doors she can no longer open. The windows are fogged. In every reflective surface, she sees him. People ask about him, she has to answer. They tell her to get a new one, she wants to kill them. Sometimes she is polite, sometimes she is not. She works. She can only walk in places posted against him, on concrete, so she withers, dulls. Sleeps as much as possible. Dreams of ash and bone, and vibrant joy, final breaths, the uncomplicated forward motion of a life lived in perfect confidence of each other. She wakes to despair.

Back west, she drives up a deadly, narrow dirt road, one lane in spots and with no guardrails against a crumbling edge and a chasm plunging hundreds of meters into a river. By the time she is at eye-level with the mountain crest across the gap, the one lined with the vast sentinel trees she'd only seen as distant, tiny markers, her ears have stopped even trying to adjust to the rapid elevation gain. A Steller's jay, close by and bunched against the rain, moves its beak in song she can't hear. When her ears pop finally, she hears Dog, there in the seat beside her, riding shotgun: he's humming. The vibration of mountain joy. The muscles covering his scapulae twitch with anticipation.

His muzzle dimples, tasting the air. She can smell him. Floral. Their joke: *Gabriel García Márquez gave you away. I can tell you are an angel by the way you smell of flowers.* She finds a place to safely pull over, sits for a long time, not looking. When she comes down again, she does it carefully.

In Indian Hollow, she asks the man if the medicine woman was Abenaki or Mohawk or some other local tribe. He doesn't know. His dog is tossing and catching a stick by himself, with great skill and hilarity. The man unloads his gun, hands it to her to examine.

"You should have one like this if you're going to be out in cat country. For bears, too," he says.

"So some say," Cecily answers. It's a strange object, meaningless to her even in her hand. "I could learn to target shoot, I suppose. But I'd never shoot a bear. Just the ground in front of it, if I had a really good reason."

"That's all you need to do, usually," he says. "Just make a big noise."

"Honestly?" She says. "If it was just me, I think I'd rather be eaten."

She does not tell him about the time she and Dog walked into a bear during a night-walk of rare true darkness: dense cloud cover, sideways winds that concealed everyone from everyone else. They'd been navigating by the feel of the dirt road underfoot, the well-known direction. So had the bear. By instinct, when muscled fur brushed her thigh and bear-musk filled her nose and Dog's, and human-dog scent filled the bear's, and they all realized what had just happened, she'd said in a loud, bright, cheerful voice like someone in a musical comedy: hello bear! Pardon us, just walking on by, have a lovely evening! Let's go, okay then! See you later! The bear huffed, but didn't hiss, and on they walked, and that was that, until they got home and collapsed on the couch in hysterical anticlimax, laughing and weepy simultaneously, their hearts scudding breakneck, a single bright sailboat.

Instead, she tells the man about the silver full moon night they were woken from sleep by a primordial sound so loud it was shaking the panes of rippled glass in the 1830's frames: a sound that erased the meaning of time and left her completely uncertain if it was the 1970's when she was a child in these deep woods, or if it was now, or the Paleolithic, but anyway, it was mating season, and the cow moose's song shook the house and her to foundation. Dog had thumped his tail in support of how moved she was, but gone back to sleep, snoring lightly: they'd hiked twelve miles of the steep Catamount Trail that day, and he was beat. She'd snuck down the cold stairs, barefoot in pools of light like mercury, but by the time she got to the door, the forest had swallowed the cow moose into itself and all was silent.

She does not tell the man about the perfect unity.

About returning to the silver-drenched bed and spooning Dog: about how within seconds, as always, their heartbeats and respiration synched.

In the east, peepers, owls, mourning doves are knives in her eardrums. Sycamore silhouettes and the small, rolling shapes of elder mountains are knives in her eyes. Trailheads buffet. Chickadees, their call his call, once the sound of home, eviscerate. Gutshot by every unremarked bee, she staggers. Falls.

She'd never had it, the Go West Young Man thing. It had irritated her. Seemed a cliché.

Now she knew: to go west is to have no memory spoor on the trail. Everything familiar, nothing the same. A sky so vast it can hold the all of it.

The next time she goes, Cecily knows, she won't come back.

Not as she was, anyway.

That person is dead.

At world's end, the stars have shaped themselves into a new constellation.

In the land of no-memory, when she looks up, it's Dog's face she sees.

Acknowledgments

With a couple of slight differences, "A More Perfect Union" appeared in *American Letters and Commentary Issue 17: Wedding the Word and the World* (New York, 2005). Gratitude to Fiction Editor Eric Darton for pulling this story from my hands and publishing it in spite of me, and to Editor in Chief Anna Rabinowitz for nominating it for a Pushcart Prize. Gratitude also to Ann Patchett and Katrina Kenison for naming it one of the "Distinguished Stories of 2005" in *The Best American Short Stories* (Houghton Mifflin: New York, 2006). I'm grateful to all the early readers, especially Jennifer Givhan for falling in love with Dog while she read and proofed the final draft.

The iridescent truth at the heart of these stories is Gilgamesh (August 13, 2001—September 9, 2013).

He happened a long time ago. He is happening now.

This book is dedicated to The Thomas J. O'Connor Animal Control and Adoption Center, and to Chuck Shaw.

About Jessamyn Smyth

Jessamyn Smyth's books *The Inugami Mochi* (2016) and *Gilgamesh Wilderness* (2021) are from Saddle Road Press. "A More Perfect Union" from *The Inugami Mochi* was selected as one of the "100 Distinguished Stories of 2005" in *Best American Short Stories* (2006). *Kitsune* is from Finishing Line Press New Women's Voices Series (2013). Her poetry and prose have appeared in *Crab Orchard Review, Taos Review, Red Rock Review, American Letters and Commentary, Nth Position, Life & Legends, Wingbeats: Exercises and Practices in Poetry,* and many other

journals and anthologies. She is the recipient of fellowships, scholarships, and grants from the Robert Francis Foundation, Bread Loaf Writer's Conference, and others. Jessamyn was the founding Editor in Chief of *Tupelo Quarterly,* and Founder/Director of the Quest Writer's Conference. She has taught Interdisciplinary Humanities and writing at Bard College Holyoke, Quest University Canada, Middlebury College, The University of Massachusetts at Amherst's Commonwealth College, The University of Pennsylvania Writer's Conference, and throughout her communities. Her books *Koan Garden* and *Skaha* are available on her website: jessamynsmyth.net.

From the Publisher

In Jessamyn Smyth's *The Inugami Mochi*, we have known the witch's expansion and joy in her familiar Beloved, and we have known the terrible end. In *Gilgamesh Wilderness*, the architecture of that great epic becomes a doorway through which the witch staggers on her mad walk west to kill death itself. Sometimes the greatest insight into what being human and mortal means comes through ancient stories and animal archetypes: in the Epic of Gilgamesh, the hero can only be made wise through loss of his wild Beloved, full knowledge of mortality, and utter humbling. What happens to us when the Beloved is not human, but instead Enkidu, panther of the wilderness? What happens when the Beloved is Humbaba's forest in a literally burning world? What happens when the Beloved is of a species co-evolved with humans for more than 80,000 years, yet constrained to a painfully short lifespan? What happens to the witch when her familiar dies? A container for meditation, eulogy, elegy, and humbling, *Gilgamesh Wilderness* is the soul cry in answer to the great human question: how do we go on, hearts open, in the presence of mortality?

Saddle Road Press hopes you'll enjoy this short excerpt from *Gilgamesh Wilderness*.

ISBN 9781736525838
Available late 2021.

www.ingramcontent.com/pod-product-compliance
Lightning Source LLC
Chambersburg PA
CBHW021023120726
47905CB00009B/3160